SUMMER COVER-UP

by

Sally Jo Pitts

Published by Gordian Books, an imprint of Winged Publications

Editor: Cynthia Hickey

Book Design by Forget Me Not Romances

Mystery and Suspense

Women sleuths

ISBN: 978-1-952661-92-1

You are my God.

Show me what you want me to do,

and let your gentle Spirit lead me in the right path.

Psalm 143:10 (CEV)

Prelude

May 10, 2002

The sound of breaking glass shattered the night silence, but no one heard it.

The homeowners were away.

Reaching inside the house, a jagged shard of glass protruding from the window frame broke off in the trespasser's arm.

The mishap required removing a glove, grasping and tossing the sharp piece of glass, then putting the glove back on.

With the press of a gloved finger, the rear door lock gave way with a click.

Broken glass crunched beneath the burglar's feet.

Stealing cash and small items of value would lead to the ultimate goal.

CHAPTER ONE

June 4, 2020

Private Investigator Jane Carson hesitated outside the Grey Investigations office located beside Robert Grey's home in Mobile, Alabama. Leftover rain plinking in the sunbaked metal gutter created a steam worthy of a barista. The buzz of a lawnmower and the scent of freshly mowed grass coming from across the street were the mundane normal in a world threatened by COVID-19.

But this morning's text from Rosemary—Send guest info ASAP—bothered Jane more than planning a wedding during a pandemic.

The stiff wedding invitation in her pocket poked her leg, prodding her to invite Robert to go with her.

Pulling the pesky card from her pocket, Jane

removed the facemask that had become everyday wearing apparel in most places and fanned her face. Only after assessing Robert's mood would she broach the wedding subject. Jane had learned to recognize the ups and downs each day's caseload presented.

She shoved the invitation back into her pocket, pulled an alcohol wipe from her purse, and cleaned the doorknob before entering the office.

Robert's eyes remained glued to his computer screen as his fingers clicked over the keyboard.

Jane pulled a baggie of homemade blueberry muffins from her purse and dropped it on his desk. "A treat to go with your morning coffee."

He stopped typing and picked up the bag. "To what do I owe baked goods?"

"Do I need to have a reason?" She did have a reason—to soften his attitude if need be—but she couldn't admit it. Not yet anyhow.

Robert shrugged. "I suppose not. The coffeepot's warming timer beeped and shut off a few minutes ago. If you want coffee, it should still be warm." He pulled a muffin from the bag. "Mmm tasty. I detect blueberries, right?"

"You do. Good detective work."

"Maybe I'm picking up your culinary ingredient identification skill."

"You're making fun."

"No, I'm not. You impressed the chef in the Costa Flores royal palace with your gift. Your palate is amazing. You still surprise me with new talents." He took another bite of muffin and returned to his typing.

Jane tugged the handbag from her shoulder, and it dropped with a *thunk* on her desk. This little office felt like home, or at least what she imagined a home should be like.

After her mother's cancer diagnosis, she had given up her apartment in Valleytown, took a year's leave from teaching, and moved to Mobile to be her caretaker and then handle her mother's affairs after she passed away. Since her mother's house and furniture had sold, Jane was left with a cot and a bare minimum of household items until the new owners moved in at the end of August.

The office was her only semblance of home now. She listened to the click of Robert's computer keys, the hum of the mini refrigerator, and smelled the aroma of strong coffee. She could hang a home sweet home sign on her desk.

But in two months, she was scheduled to report to her teaching job in Valleytown. Though she had an obligation, she still had the nudging to pray for direction. God has plans for his people. If only he would send a text, spelling out her next steps. She'd love the assurance that she was on the right track.

For now, she had a place to belong, relax and share ideas and concerns ... at least most concerns. The letter in her pocket generated a heat.

She retrieved the *I Spy* mug Robert gave her after

their recent royal adventure in the Caribbean and went to the coffeepot.

"What is the order of business today?"

"Catching up on case files. I need yesterday's report on the Braxton surveillance." He hole-punched pages and placed them in a folder. "It's hot and muggy outside. Aren't you glad you aren't cooped up in your car watching him through fogged up windows today?"

"Uh-huh."

Robert looked up; a pencil stuck behind his ear. "Is that all you have to say? I thought I'd at least receive an enthusiastic 'that's great' from my coworker who loves to look at the bright side."

"Sorry." She reeled in her wandering thoughts. "Mr. Braxton is a good actor. He limped out on the Dog River dock using his cane and suddenly didn't need it after he caught a big fish."

Jane sipped coffee and wrinkled her nose. "This stuff tastes like burnt shoe leather."

"You know how burnt shoe leather tastes?"

She gave him a lopsided grin. "I do now." Jane added sugar and made the brew taste like sweetened mud. Returning to her desk, she turned on her computer and pulled the notepad from her purse containing the notes from the Braxton Workman's Comp case.

The office phone rang, and Robert answered.

If she assisted Robert in finishing the case file, she could take advantage of his good spirit and he might be more open to attending the wedding with her. Jane slipped the invitation from her pocket and reread the attached letter from Rosemary.

With the Stay-at-Home order amended to Safer-at-Home guidelines, the wedding at the lodge is a go!! And I owe it all to you, my maid of honor, and your suggestions.

The lodge agreed to CDC sanitation regulations. We'll limit in-person attendance to the wedding party and guests who consent to testing and quarantine prior to arrival, and we will offer a virtual option.

Cecelia, Arnold, and Evan are coming. Darin agreed to be Phillip's best man and Arnold as a notary agreed to perform the ceremony.

Since our group is small, everyone can bring a guest who follows the safety guidelines. We'll be one big family. Valley Voices (and Shooting Stars) will shine again!

Jane smiled at the memory of the Shooting Stars—the exclusive club started in 6th grade with three members: Rosemary, Cecelia and Jane.

The rest of the letter went over the safety details, but Jane's eyes rested on the words *bring a guest.* Rosemary said Evan Armstrong, her sometime boyfriend in high school and assistant principal at Hidden Valley Elementary, was bringing a teacher as his guest. Cecelia and Arnold were married. Darin, who dumped her, had his socialite wife to accompany him, leaving Jane solo.

Not that solo was so bad, but it would be uncomfortable. She'd been to affairs over the years and seen the pitying looks. It's usual for the members of the wedding party to attend with a date. If you went alone, the assumption is you couldn't get a date. Jane shifted in her chair and tried another sip of the foul coffee. She certainly didn't need to be attached to anyone to be of value. But still, she didn't want to appear to be a pitiful, boyfriendless, unattached specimen, making table placements uneven.

She glanced at Robert, intent in conversation on the phone. She liked the way his chin set when concentrating. He was kind, thoughtful, a good listener, believed in giving a client his best effort, and had risked taking her on as a novice investigator. But would all those good attributes stretch to being a sort of date at a wedding weekend?

No denying there had been sparks between them and they had kissed, but they agreed to pretend it never happened and to keep their relationship professional.

So … what would it hurt for him to play the role of her date ... a temp boyfriend just for the wedding weekend. This was for Rosemary. Her fellow Shooting Star. Jane sketched a star on her desk pad with her finger. She would not let her down.

Something bumped Jane's arm. Robert. He placed a bottle of vitamin water in front of her.

"Try this. Maybe it will bring you back to earth. I've been talking to you."

"Sorry." She took the chilled bottle. She should use it to cool her flushed face. "I thought you were still on the phone."

He set a paper on the desk. "You left this museum curator job description in the copy tray. Is curator Braxton's job?"

"No. He's a field service tech for a cleaning company. I was searching for the job requirements when I saw the museum listing with the Department of Archives and History. I couldn't resist copying the description."

"Fine, but I need your surveillance report. I'm working on the summary page now."

"I'm on it." Jane grabbed her notepad. "I was looking for a pen."

"If a pen is what you need, here you go." He pulled one from his pocket and handed it to her.

Heat filled her cheeks. She was self-absorbed and neglecting her duties. For the next twenty minutes, she willed herself to focus on her surveillance notes. She transcribed the number of times Mr. Braxton knelt, squatted, and stooped and included a narration of the video of him walking on the long pier carrying a heavy load with his cane tucked under his arm and compared these capabilities with the duties and requirements of the job he held when injured.

"Here ya' go." She poked the send button. "Check

my report to see if I've covered everything."

"Back at you with the summary I wrote for you to proof."

"I feel bad for the guy," Jane said. "Workers' Compensation doesn't want to pay undeserved wages, but the guy may have pushed himself physically yesterday and suffered for it when he got home."

"Workers' Comp needs to know if his on-the-job injury is sufficiently disabling to prevent returning to work. We observe and give facts. We don't provide tests, like a doctor or therapist might, to confirm need. Our job is to report what we see them do in their natural environment."

She understood, but still wondered. Is what we see, or think we see, really the whole story? After reviewing and making a few grammatical corrections, Jane said, "The summary is ready." She sent the shared document back to him.

Robert nodded. "I like what you did in your report, adding the physical requirements of Braxton's job to compare to the specific abilities you observed. You and research. I can see you sinking your teeth into the museum job."

"It's just a dream." She patted the museum curator job description he'd laid on her desk. "I suspect the museum job will go to someone in-house."

"Never know."

His trace of a smile and bit of encouragement fueled her real dream—to continue to work with him.

However, she was stuck with teaching. She'd been given a year's leave to tend to her mother's affairs and was to return to the classroom in August. Her kindergarten students were sweet but following new state mask and social distancing rules and possible virtual learning would make for a new world at school. At least opening day was ten weeks away. Rosemary's wedding was in less than three weeks. She needed to bring a guest, and Robert was in business mode.

"I'll work on the invoice," Robert said, "if you'll pull the copies from the printer and hand me a report cover."

Jane gathered the papers from the printer and went to the supply cabinet. Maybe her brother would go with her to the wedding. No. He was still recovering from his kidney transplant. Besides, going with her brother would paint "loser" across her forehead. Her only option was Robert. How could she approach him so he wouldn't say no and close his mind?

He was in a good mood with the Braxton report completed. She reflected on the morning's devotion which spoke of looking for God's guidance in decisions big and small. She had prayed. Everything pointed to asking Robert, but what to say was the next hurdle. *Lord, here goes.*

She grabbed a red file folder for courage, took a deep breath, and turned to face Robert seated at his desk. "Will you be my friend?" she blurted.

He looked up from punching buttons on his

calculator.

"Be your friend? I thought I was your friend." He ran his fingers down a row of figures on the time and expense log.

"I mean as a boy ... you know … as my employer, who is a boy and a friend but not a boyfriend. But maybe seems to be a boyfriend." She closed her eyes and winced. "At a wedding."

Robert sat frozen with one hand on the calculator and the other on his time sheet. His brows knit together, then he picked up the plastic bag of blueberry muffins and dangled it. "Aha," he said, and smirked.

Jane lifted her chin. "I had blueberries begging me to do something with them. I would have made those wedding or not."

"Okay. I'm a friend and I appreciate the muffins but not enough to get me to a wedding." He returned to his numbers.

"But you see, here's the deal. Rosemary and Phillip, the bride and groom, went to high school with me. They dated all through high school before he went into the military. He's stationed back in the States after three tours in Afghanistan. They set a date months ago—before the pandemic. I promised to be her maid of honor."

"Why not go virtual like others are doing?"

"The parents and other guests will be there virtually on Zoom. But she wants her high school chorus friends who will make up the wedding party to be there in person."

"You go."

"But single wedding participants are to bring a guest. I worked with Rosemary on pandemic safety precautions. The event will be at Eaglemont Lodge in north Alabama near Lookout Mountain. We will become a family group; the way football teams are planning to do for the fall season. I've invited Mr. Sing, our chorus teacher, and his wife as a surprise if they are willing to follow the virus prevention safeguards. The wedding will be a treasured time for my closest friends and—"

"You don't want to show up without a date."

Jane bit at her lower lip and nodded.

"I thought Lookout Mountain was in Tennessee."

"It is. But the mountain has sides in Georgia and Alabama. Wouldn't you love to see it?"

She pulled the invitation from her pocket with the letter attached and pointed to the map of the lodge's location and placed it on his desk. Robert reached for the letter. Was he softening?

He read, and then a grin slowly spread across his face. "Correct me if I'm wrong, but aren't Evan and Darin old flames of yours?"

"More like sparks than flames. I dated Evan in high school and Darin in college."

"I see. And would this need for a friend who is a boy be to play the role of setting these old sparks on their heels? I show them what they missed out on so they will kick themselves for ever letting you go?"

She felt her face warm.

"No need to answer." He flicked his hand in the air. "They should kick themselves."

"Does that mean you'll go?"

"Tell you what. I'll give you the time off. Ask Mr. Braxton here," Robert pointed to the reports on his desk, "to do it. He has proven to be a good actor."

~

Robert shifted his gaze from the letter in his hand to Jane's flushed face. Her head lowered and shoulders drooped. A pang of regret shot through him. He'd been mean to taunt her, especially since he didn't want her going anywhere with someone else.

She was asking him to play the role of an employer who had no interest in her along romantic lines. In truth, he had to play that role daily. He had to squash the urge to tug a stray lock of hair from her cheek or to tap her nose when she wrinkled it at him in playful frustration. He'd learned how to social distance from Jane weeks ahead of the governor's Safer-at-Home mandates.

And there was no need to pretend there was nothing between them because, unfortunately, there was nothing going on between them. If it would help her standing with her friends, he should be there for her. Hadn't she stepped in and done everything asked of her in the agency and more? She had been willing to play pretend roles when situations called for it. Suffering through a weekend with her old high school friends was the least he could do.

Yet if he was reading her right. She wanted people to suspect there was more to the relationship than they were saying. Could he manage the ruse? If pretending put them in close proximity, it would truly be taxing his will power. Evidently, the deception would be no problem for her. The more he thought about it, the more intriguing the challenge.

He set the letter down. "How do you do a wedding in a pandemic with no hugging and handshaking?"

"Everyone has agreed to take precautionary measures by testing fourteen days out, quarantining at home and then testing again the day of departure. If everyone is free of the virus and then confine ourselves to the mountain lodge, we should be safe to associate. We'll take food, clothes and supplies, so there will be no need to come and go. And it will be nice to reminisce with real people and not images on a screen."

Robert shook his head. "It seems logical to wait instead of going to all this trouble."

"They've waited long enough, eighteen years. Phillip has been in the military on remote duty assignments and Rosemary was needed to run the family's restaurant business in Valleytown because of her father's long-term illness. As soon as we learned Phillip would finish his twenty years of service at Maxwell Air Force Base, Rosemary, Cecelia and I began talking about wedding plans. Then the pandemic struck. Since we've devised a way to deal with the virus, I would hate to let her down. So, what do you say?"

He pointed to the agency calendar on his desk. "I have to check our workload. The child custody case is on the first and third weekends."

"The third weekend may be a nonissue if the judge approves halting weekend shuffling because of coronavirus concerns."

"We have to check on the traveling salesman now that the Stay-At-Home orders have been lifted."

"I'll talk to his wife, but last I knew she said he might continue to work from home for a while. And the Braxton case is complete with the report I just sent you."

He pulled a mailing label from his desk drawer, opened the file, and copied the client's address. Hand me a larger mailer, will you? Looking up, he was confronted with Jane's lifted brows and shining, hopeful eyes.

"So, if we're free that weekend you'll go?"

"I'll ... think about it." And he would.

"Sure. Think about it … you should."

He was hedging, and she knew it. He'd learned the clues of how to read and react to her, just as she had him. He knew when to be quiet and listen to a tirade. Or to draw out her thoughts when she went silent. Like now.

The agency had become a twosome, and they worked well together. She helped him think through and come to solutions by picking up on investigative clues. What would he do without her? He would have to re-acclimate as a one-man agency. But what if she were to stay? Was it possible? Would his feelings for her continue to sneak up and tap him on the shoulder and hint at romance?

She laid the mailing envelope on his desk.

Robert attached the label and rubber stamped it with the office return address.

Jane held out her hand. "I'll take it to the post office and pick up fresh coffee. The batch you made this morning was stale or something."

"I just dumped what was left in the bottom of the bag. Not my greatest attempt at coffee making. When you return, pull up your notes on the child custody case. I want to be certain we've addressed each issue on the attorney's list of concerns. He tapped his calendar; the mother is to pick up the five-year-old at five o'clock. Since the governor opened restaurants, bars, and breweries with social distancing, we need to see if she goes out."

Jane's keys rattled as she fished them out of her purse, grabbed the envelope, and headed to the door. "I've got my blend-in-the-bar-crowd cap and shirt ready. We'll see if she steps out tonight. It's a shame parents can't stand back and unselfishly ask themselves, 'How can we work together to keep our child safe?'"

"Too sensible. Something human nature doesn't allow for."

"Proof of the fall of man?"

"Could be."

"I'll be back shortly," she said, closing the door behind her.

The time was nearing when she would close the door for good and not return. Nothing would be the same. He wanted her to stay, but she had other plans. He knew that from the start.

She was leaving to return to her teaching job in a couple of months. But he was used to working with her now. She was like fresh air sweeping into an abandoned house, water to a wilted plant, aspirin to a headache, a lifeboat to a sinking ship.

He liked to think she needed him, too. At least he'd rescued her from not only dangerous situations, but personal problems. He liked being needed, especially by her. It felt real and right. The agency would not be the same, but it would be selfish to ask her to stay. He wished he could offer the health and pension benefits of the teaching job.

Her work here was temporary. He had to accept it and move on. To what, he didn't know. All he really knew was law enforcement. PI work skirted around the fringes but was not real police work with authority and resources. He had to rely on his former colleague for assistance.

Robert heaved a sigh. He'd spent twenty-five years as a lawman before he retired. At forty-four, it was too late to turn back. He pushed away from his desk, picked up his cup and rinsed it in the sink. Why in the world drink this mess if it tasted so bad? Habit? Comfort? Something to do with his hands? Why put sludge into your body? Why do drug addicts continue to do things that they wish they didn't? Why in the world consider going to a wedding in the middle of a pandemic?

He lifted his wife, Lori's framed watercolor of a sunset on Mobile Bay from the shelf over the sink. It was nearing three years since Lori died of cancer. Her death was one of a series of losses in his life. He lost his job, his good name as a lawman, and his wife within months of each other. Technically, he didn't lose his job. He retired. But his superiors with the State Bureau of Investigation were relieved. When accusations and circumstances were explained and he was vindicated of fraud, he was asked to return. But the damage to his reputation had been done, and he'd already opened the agency.

Now he faced the pending loss of Jane. Even the family cancer support group where he had met Jane was folding due to COVID-19. The attempt at meeting virtually didn't foster the same closeness and sympathetic support.

Private investigations in a pandemic world weren't the same. People stayed home and didn't sneak around, meeting in bars or back corners of restaurants. Cheatin' spouses' style had been cramped. Workers had no places of employment to go to and employers quit hiring, so there were no backgrounds to run. Curtailing exchange of children in shared custody was likely. This could be the ideal time for a getaway at a mountain lodge even if it included a wedding. Could he handle it? He returned Lori's painting to the shelf and picked up the coffee carafe with the thick scorched remains. Pouring it out, he ran water in the sink and watched the black contents swirl and thin to a light brown until the water in the sink ran clear.

Maybe in the mountain air, clear of the virus as possible, he could think about where to go next with his life. Robert was an investigator and knew how to list and examine facts. Why not use the technique now?

He grabbed a blank sheet of paper from the printer and returned to his desk. He made two columns. Why and why not go with Jane to the lodge.

He'd start with, why not.

1. Pandemic
2. Don't like weddings
3. Have to dress up
4. Be with bunch of people don't know
5. Five hours away
6. Be expected to dance
7. Inviting temptation

His grandpa once gave him good advice. If you don't want to get caught in the undertow, stay out of the water. Getting close to Jane was risky, especially on moonlit nights. He'd already succumbed to kissing Jane once, and they both agreed to forget it and keep things between them professional. Would play-acting be smart? He might be begging for another loss—loss of a relationship that could never happen.

He shifted to the why column.

1. Case work should be caught up
2. Jane asked him
3. Wouldn't have to worry about how she was doing and if she was staying safe
4. Use time to regroup and decide where to go next with the agency
5. Be fun showing Evan and Darin what schmucks they were for letting her go

He was running out of space. Opening his desk drawer for more paper, he came face to face with his morning devotion book and set it on his desk.

Today's subject had touched on seeking God's guidance. He reread a Scripture from Proverbs 19. In the commentary, the writer concluded when making decisions—big or small—we should seek wisdom from Scripture, godly counsel and the leading of the Holy Spirit.

Placing his hands over the list, he prayed. *Lord, these are my thoughts, and we are expected to use our common sense. But in this matter, show me what I should do. I'd appreciate direction about Jane's request.*

He bowed and listened, hoping the answer would come before Jane returned. He waited. His mind wandered to Jane and her enthusiasm for work, her determination to do a good job for him, and her dedication to learn the investigation rules he gave her. It made him smile to think of the rule list she kept in her handbag along with her camera, binoculars, sunglasses, caps, T-shirt, and other accessories for ready disguises. His mind stayed on Jane when he heard her car pull into the drive.

No clear answer, Lord?

Was the length of his lists the answer? The why nots were longer. Or was he supposed to wait?

The door opened, and Jane held up a new bag of coffee. "Mission accomplished." She deposited the coffee beside the coffeepot. "Should I make a fresh pot?"

"If you want. I gave up and poured the black tar out."

"Good idea."

She busied herself at the coffeemaker, and Robert lifted Jane's invitation letter. "This Mr. Sing you mentioned inviting, is he Asian?"

Jane giggled. "Mr. Sing was the nickname for our chorus teacher, Mr. Singletary. He selected six of us to perform as an ensemble and we put on performances all over the area."

"Tillman's Crossing with one caution light produced a traveling ensemble?"

"Tillman's Crossing is just a small farm community where I lived with my grandma. I went to school in Valleytown."

"Valleytown High School?"

Jane clamped the lid onto the glass carafe and pressed the brew button. “Sure did. Class of 2002.”

“Your chorus teacher’s wife was found murdered in their home?”

Jane turned and used a clip to secure the coffee bag. “Yes. How did you know?”

“Your Mr. Sing remains the prime suspect.”

CHAPTER TWO

Mr. Singletary? Murderer? Surely Robert wasn't serious.

"You worked the case in Valleytown?" Jane asked.

"I was a new state agent assigned to work the murder with another officer from the Alabama Bureau of Investigation's criminal division. The Veronica Singletary murder remains my only unsolved homicide. The case is technically still open."

"Just think, we were in the same town at the same time. Everyone said Mrs. Singletary was the victim of a burglary. How does that make Mr. Sing the prime suspect?"

"I had my doubts about it being a burglary. Still do."

"Was Mr. Singletary automatically a suspect because he was the spouse?"

Robert didn't respond. Instead, he wrinkled his brow

and wrote on a paper on his desk.

Jane persisted. "Am I right?"

He looked up. "About what?"

Jane huffed. Was he trying to annoy her? "About suspecting the husband when the wife is a murder victim being routine."

He finished writing and tapped the open devotion book on his desk.

She hadn't noticed it there earlier. Had he been studying it while she was gone? They each had copies of the same devotional and the topic today had stressed listening to and accepting responsible instruction to gain wisdom.

"It depends. Every case is different."

"In this case, everyone in school said she walked in on a burglar who killed her." Jane steepled her hands beneath her chin. "The entire school grieved for him. Remarkably, he was able to pull himself together and finish out the school year."

"No doubt."

Jane flung her hands out wide. "What do you mean by that?"

"Just what I said. No doubt he'd pull up his bootstraps and endear himself to his students and peers. He may have been purposely playing on people's sympathies."

"Or maybe he was devastated, truly courageous, and put on a brave face for his students," she said, fisting her hands on her hips.

"Look. As you can see, it might be dicey and put a damper on the festivities if I show up at this wedding affair."

She eyed the devotional. "Or there might be a reason for this opportunity." Her high school friends would share good things about their teacher. And if Mr. Singletary did arrange to come, Robert would see what a nice person he was and couldn't be the culprit. She'd dangle a carrot. If he came, maybe he'd find a clue to solve the cold case.

"Did you actually question Mr. Singletary?"

"The lead investigator handled his initial questioning. I played the role of observer, but I did talk to him and others during the investigation. I'd have to review the case to remember the details."

"Chances are the murder won't even be mentioned," Jane said, "but my high school friends coming to this wedding were all around at the time of the murder and may shed some light on the case for you."

"If the subject comes up, I don't want to put people on edge."

"You won't. Please come." She pointed to the devotion on his desk. "Doesn't the Bible say something about this day having enough to worry about without worrying about tomorrow? You are worrying about an issue that may be a non-issue."

Robert pursed his lips, held the pen with his thumb and jiggled it against his fingers for a moment before setting it down. "You have a point." He took out his phone. “Pull out both of the current case files and make sure they’re up to date while I make a call.”

Jane flipped open the traveling salesman folder to the time and service sheet clipped in the front. She still needed to type up her notes from a phone conversation with the wife and update the invoice. In the child custody case, the weekend surveillance reports needed to be typed and to figure the time and mileage for the invoice.

If there was a perfect time for a getaway as far as the agency workload, it was now.

The coffeemaker beeped, signaling the completed brew cycle. Jane poured a cup for Robert and herself. The aroma and color fresher in contrast to the dregs she’d tried earlier.

She set the cup next to him and he mouthed a thanks before speaking into the phone. “Hi Vance. Are you working in the office or on the road?”

She took a sip of coffee. While he talked to his friend at the State Bureau of Investigation, Jane glanced at the paper on Robert’s desk divided into why and why not sections. She was glad to see he was putting thought into her invitation. She smiled when she saw he had placed “might have to dance” in the why not column. She’d learned he was an excellent dancer only three months ago when he had twirled the Queen of Costa Flores around the palace ballroom dance floor. He’d penciled in “murder case” with a question mark underneath both columns. Interesting. He saw the cold case could be a reason for and against going to the wedding weekend.

She returned to her desk, tuning into Robert's end of the phone conversation.

"Do you think I can get a copy of the Singletary murder case?"

What was he doing? Would he stir up discord? She wanted to create a joyful occasion for Rosemary and Phillip. Why had she said revisiting the investigation would be of no concern? In honesty, the murder was a shock she had managed to block from her thoughts. But Robert's mention of Mr. Singletary as a suspect opened the door she had kept closed for eighteen years.

Jane had been tired after returning from the tri-county high school chorus performance the night before. She'd failed to set her alarm and overslept.

Running to beat the tardy bell, she snatched the choir room door open and was startled by what she saw.

With graduation only six school days away, Mr. Sing had stressed these last days of practice were critical to giving the seniors a proper sendoff. The choir was to sing the national anthem and the alma mater at the graduation ceremony. The room should have been filled with smiling faces and enthusiasm. Instead, there were slumped shoulders, puffy faces and sniffling noses.

Principal Haywood Jones stood at the teacher's podium. The seating normally arranged—with sopranos in front progressing to tenor, alto and bass on the back row—was all jumbled up. The close-knit group of seniors clustered together. Rosemary clutched Phillip's hand; her face streaked with tears. Evan, Darin, and Arnold, leaned against the desk at the front of the room, heads down. Only Cecelia was missing from the ensemble group. A tingle niggled the back of Jane's neck. Something tragic had happened. Principal Jones motioned to Jane.

"Yes sir?"

"Mr. Singletary is out today; his wife was found dead in their home last night."

Jane's mind went numb. Mr. Jones instructed everyone to take seats and called the roll. Jane sat in the front row, her heart aching for their teacher. The numbness finally gave way to tears. She fished in her backpack and pulled out tissues. She dabbed at her eyes with one hand and held up the tissue packet in the other and could feel the brush of hands taking advantage of the offer.

"Hearts are heavy for Mr. Singletary. I brought a roll of banner paper for you to express your condolences."

Reflecting on that day, Jane was grateful for the way Principal Jones had handled the class.

The memory of the closing verses of the senior song, co-written by Cecelia and Mr. Sing, still struck the chords of her heart and sent chills running through her:

Valleytown High your teachings
Will ring forever true,
We'll always band together,
The Class of Two-Thousand-Two.

"Jane?"

Robert's voice broke through the cheers and standing ovation from classmates, teachers, administrators, parents, relatives, and friends at graduation.

"You're looking mighty sad over there."

"High school memories."

"This teacher at your high school. What did you think of him?"

"As a teacher or murder suspect?"

"Both."

"He was the best teacher I ever had. And I could never see him as capable of committing murder."

Robert pressed his lips into a thin line and gave a single nod. His response said he appreciated her candor, though he might not agree.

"Are you looking to reopen the case of his wife's murder?"

"An unsolved murder case is never closed. I would like to review the names of those I spoke to in case it comes up but ... if you'd rather I didn't attend—"

"No. I want you there." Jane bit at her lower lip. "But sitting here reliving the morning after the murder when we all found out ... you're right. It might make people uncomfortable to have the murder come up. I also understand you want to refresh your memory and review the case ... but can you be discreet?"

"I'm an expert at hush-hush operations but if someone remembers me—"

Jane pushed out of her chair and clapped her hands.

"Does that mean you'll go?"

"My primary purpose shall be to go as your employer whom your friends will likely suspect is your boyfriend. But I will fiercely deny any such attachment, which will make your buddies further believe there must be something beyond friends to our relationship … and I'll keep my cold case interests under wraps."

Jane put on her happy face, tamping down her own qualms. She hadn't heard from Mr. Singletary and maybe his ignoring her invitation was for the best. She no longer had to attend the wedding solo. With Robert at her side, what could go wrong?

~

The officer who led the way to the cold case evidence locker in Montgomery had introduced himself as a retired rehire. The flatfoot label hung on policemen suited him as his feet slapped the floor along the long hallway. He wore a facemask, per CDC recommendations, and spoke over his shoulder in a muffled voice.

"I ... uniform ... forty ... couldn't shed ... habit."

Robert gathered the officer was explaining he'd spent forty years as a uniformed officer. Had this man done something stupid and been forced to retire instead of being fired?

No ... that was his story.

Robert contemplated his own twenty-five years spent honing his skills as an investigator who was now reduced to watching parents and small children riding on the merry-go-round of shared custody swaps and skulking behind suspected wayward spouses. He had been good at his lawman job ... except for the day he mistakenly deposited ten thousand dollars of informant cash in his personal bank account, spent it and was charged with grand theft.

The charge did not include the extenuating circumstances. He had been exhausted, working long hours on a drug detail where the informant was a no show, leaving him with cash he didn't want on him over the weekend. What little sleep he had managed was in a lightly padded straight-back chair in a hospital room. He had listened to the incessant beeps of monitoring and dispensing machines, watching his wife slip away from him as cancer took its toll on her body. He wrote checks to pay bills. Wasn't that how it was done? Lori had always handled their finances.

Bundled like a phone-internet-cable package offer, he accepted a deal for early retirement. Losing his good name was a bonus.

Though the money was repaid, and he was eventually cleared of the charge due to Jane's investigative work—which was another story—being rid of the taint proved to be like unshooting a gun. It didn't work.

The bottom of his shoes clicked against the waxed floor. The bleak surroundings and gray walls might depress some people, but to Robert the environment wrapped him in a cocoon of law enforcement comfort and stirred his investigative juices. The officer opened the heavy security fire door and stepped aside for Robert to enter. Inside, Robert inhaled the remnants of justice undelivered. Ironically the cool, climate-controlled room housed the investigative puzzle pieces of cold cases if pulled and fitted together in just the right pattern might earn the stamp of *case cleared.*

The officer clucked his tongue. “These cases are relegated to shelves in a cave-like existence and locked up. It seems cruel for the victims and the victims’ families and our communities. The folks deserve closure.” He made a sweeping gesture toward the rows and rows of boxes. “It makes my day to think a new fact has come to light to warrant further investigation. Good luck, sir. I hope a new set of eyes on a case will change the status from open to closed.”

He left. The clang of the door echoed in the cavernous room, holding the muffled screams of unfathomable tragedies. Steel shelving units were brimming with labeled evidence boxes filled with fingerprint cards, clothing, and anything a suspect might have touched to provide clues to untold murders and other atrocities.

As the officer suggested, maybe a new set of eyes could help ferret out the truth. In this instance, instead of a new set of eyes, he was bringing the same set of eyes. But they were older eyes with more experience behind them.

Robert had the location numbers for the Singletary

murder Vance had given him earlier.

"I've cleared the way for you to go to the evidence locker and review and copy what you need," Vance had said. "The chief has discussed forming a cold case squad to make periodic reviews of cases. Sometimes, data overlooked can be spotted or new information might be available. Do I have to remind you that cold case investigations is exactly where I know you should be?"

Robert had started to interrupt, but Vance continued.

"You worry about your tarnished reputation, but you're not the first to mess up, nor will you be the last. At least think about working unsolved crimes."

"Hold the enthusiasm. Let's see what is accomplished with a review of the Singletary homicide. Several of the people who were questioned regarding the murder will be at the gathering Jane wants me to attend. My purpose in examining the file is to freshen my memory of the details of the crime and who I talked to. But I'd be less than honest if I didn't admit I am also interested in a resolution. The Veronica Singletary homicide is the only unsolved murder on my record. I'll look at what was done and what was left undone. With new forensic techniques and looking at the file with experience I didn't have then ... who knows?"

"Not to beat a dead horse but do me a favor ... do everyone a favor … and think about working with us to make the cold case unit a reality."

"Are you in a bartering mood?"

"Always," Vance said.

"I'll think about your request if you will check on the status of the Museum Curator of Education job with the Alabama Department of Archives and History."

"Have you acquired hidden talents you've never shared?"

"Jane is panting over this job. I'd like to see her have a chance at it."

"I thought she was going back to teaching kindergarten."

"She is, but I know this type of work is something she'd love. The job would also include insurance and retirement benefits. Perks I can't offer her or I'd ask her to stay on with the agency."

"Consider your barter proposal a done deal."

Robert walked along rows and rows of shelves, standing back-to-back, separated by walk-through spaces. He read the labels of cases until he spotted Row J shelf 1 locations 3a, and 3b of case #ABI-44-005242002. The gun associated with the case number was stored in a separate gun locker area.

He pulled a fat three-ring notebook, called the murder book, from one of the storage boxes. His pulse quickened as he flipped to the cover page with the one-sentence synopsis:

The decedent is a 25-year-old married female who was found by her husband in the kitchen of their home with a gunshot wound to the chest.

Staring at the photos of the crime scene, a shiver ran

through him. He was breathing air denied Veronica Singletary. She lay on the floor, blood from a cut on her head had run onto her headband. Her blouse had another bloody stain. What had happened? What was the last thing she saw? Did she see the killer? Did she know the killer? Terror and suffering were her last companions.

He turned to the summary page with the conclusion written by him eighteen years ago:

The circumstances resulting in the victim's death are apparently due to an interrupted burglary involving an unknown assailant.

Investigation status: Open

Veronica Singletary was taken from this world too soon. She has no voice now, but her silent cry for justice still deserves to be heard. She deserves closure.

CHAPTER THREE

Robert at the wheel of Jane's car, handed the Hardee's drive-thru order to Jane, who used disinfecting towelettes to wipe off the cups and food bag. The antiseptic smell of the wipes combined with the spicy aroma of sausage biscuits and the car freshener. "There's hand sanitizer in the door pocket." Jane said.

"I thought wiping bags and containers wasn't necessary since the virus spreads mainly through the respiratory droplets people spray when talking, coughing, and such," Robert said.

"It won't hurt to take extra care."

"Extra care would be to not host or attend a wedding during a pandemic."

"It's not so bad. Safer-at-Home state guidelines are old hat for a kindergarten teacher. To keep the little ones germ free, I constantly issued reminders to respect each other's personal space, cough and sneeze into the elbow, and sing "Happy Birthday" while scrubbing hands to ensure enough time is spent cleansing."

Robert pulled to one side out of the drive-thru and used the sanitizer in the door pocket to clean his hands.

Jane wasn't about to comment on his quips about attending the wedding. He had been a champ about being tested and retested for the virus and using store and fast-food deliveries. They'd used the self-imposed quarantine time in the office to clean and update files. He'd also been reading his copy of the Singletary murder book but had not talked about it.

"Do you have any new revelations in the murder case? What can you do after so many years have passed? Are there other officers who have reviewed the case? Do you want a wipe for the steering wheel?"

Robert held up his hand, palm outward. "Yes, to new revelations. Several things can be done. No other officers reviewed. And yes, I'll use a wipe on the steering wheel. If this is a memory test, I hope I passed."

Jane poked straws into the juice drink lids and sighed. "I must sound crazy. Want to know the truth?"

"Please."

"I'm nervous about the murder investigation coming up." She had been jittery since she invited Robert to join her for the weekend and then learned he suspected her former teacher had murdered his wife.

"I told you it might be best if I didn't attend. It's not too late. Just drop me off at my house."

"No." Jane tightened her lips. "You can't back out now. You promised if all the agency cases were caught up ... and they are ... you'd go with me."

"I did promise, and you've done an admirable job. So, I'm sticking to my bargain. But if my going is making you freaky, won't your boyfriend agenda be defeated?"

"I don't have an agenda, it's just ..."

"Just what? You're supposed to be giving me truth."

"You see the dashboard on my car?"

"I do. It appears nice and clean."

"I had the car washed, and the interior cleaned for this trip."

"I hope you didn't go to the trouble for me."

"I wanted the car clean so we could have a fresh start on the trip."

"Okay. Nice idea. So, should we not eat in the car and mess it up?"

"Eating in the car is fine. I want you to do the same with the murder case."

"Eat it?"

"No silly. To start fresh ... to have an open mind ... not judge Mr. Sing guilty ahead of time."

"Truth?"

She rolled her eyes and slumped against the seat back. "Please."

"I have read over the file and I am looking at it from

a different point of view. It's been eighteen years and it would be sad if my investigative abilities hadn't improved. Glaring holes jumped out at me. Things were left undone. There are new technologies available to further examine the evidence collected. In essence, I am looking at the case with fresh eyes."

"Really?" Jane had sensed a new energy in Robert since he had begun reading the old case book. She wanted him to be successful. Viewing cold cases might be his calling. But she didn't want him to succeed at the expense of her teacher. "So, you don't think Mr. Singletary murdered his wife?"

"I can't say. The point is, I have learned lessons since the murder—policies I've been teaching you."

Jane sat upright. "Like, don't jump to conclusions?"

"Yes. And things are not always as they seem."

She turned toward him. "To work just as hard to prove a man's innocence as his guilt?"

He leveled intense blue-gray eyes on her. "And remember everyone is a suspect until they are not a suspect."

Jane tapped the car instrument panel. "Clean slate just like my dashboard?"

"All clean." He dusted his hands together. "Do you have the address for the lodge?"

"I do." Jane took a sip of her juice, letting it cool her throat and pulled her notepad from her purse. "Two fourteen Mountain Air Circle, Kingsboro."

Robert entered the address for directions on his

phone and placed it on the center console. "We have four and a half hours. I'm shifting to objective mode. You know the players in the case and were there at the time. I want you to look at the file and give me your thoughts. Then I'll shelve the case for the weekend and play the part of your non-boyfriend. If the case comes up, it won't be by me."

"Thank you. You're a lifesaver." Jane's nerves calmed and her heart warmed in appreciation for Robert's willingness to shield her wallflower insecurity and pigeonhole the cold case.

"You've stepped up to the plate for me. I'll make the sacrifice and endure a weekend at a mountain top lodge in the fresh summer air for you."

"That doesn't sound exactly equal," Jane said with a pout.

"Hey, add that the martyrdom of the trip includes: a wedding during a pandemic, chitchat with people I don't know, walking a tightrope dealing with your old boyfriends while pretending to be a non-boyfriend/boyfriend—"

Jane threw up both hands. "Okay. Enough already. We're even."

Robert grinned and pulled onto the highway, headed toward the northbound I-65 ramp. "I could use a sausage biscuit."

Jane peeled back the wrapper, handed him a biscuit with a napkin, then bit into the fluffy goodness of her own biscuit. Her phone beeped with a text message.

She read and huffed a sigh of relief. “The last report I was waiting to receive. Cecelia and Arnold both tested negative and will be on their way. I can mark them off on my maid of honor checklist I created.” Jane held up her phone with the app.

“What? No notepad?”

“I still like to write on a notepad, but this checklist has come in handy.”

“How do you know so much about bridesmaids and wedding responsibilities?”

“Experience. Bridesmaid times four and maid of honor times two.”

“Isn’t there a bad luck saying about always a bridesmaid never a bride?”

“There is.” Jane opened a grape jelly packet and squeezed it on her biscuit. “Supposedly if you serve as a bridesmaid more than twice, you may never marry.”

“Must be where the term ‘old maid’ comes from.” Robert turned and winked at her.

The wink did not sit well with her. “To label someone as doomed to singleness is unfair just because they have lots of friends who deem them special to stand at their wedding.”

“I agree. It’s wrong to make a girl feel like she is being left behind when all her friends are marrying. The saying may have been born from insecurities. Maybe catching the bouquet negates the curse.”

“Yeah. Maybe.” Jane swallowed her own insecurities and washed them down with the rest of her juice. “Some of the silly old wives’ tales make a girl feel second rate but I choose not to overthink it and enjoy the traditions.”

“Tossing bouquets, old maids—why not just find a justice of the peace, say ‘I do’, and be done with it?”

“Just the way it is.” Jane shoved her phone with the checklist back in her purse. “Some rites of passage require a celebration.” She reached for the murder book. “You asked me to review this case.”

“Wait until you finish eating. I don’t want jelly sticking up the pages.”

“Yes sir. Something sweet reminds me of another tradition: eating Chilton County peaches in the summer. Watch for a place to pick up a basket on the way.” She pulled out the facemask she kept tucked in her purse. “I’ll use my mask and social distance.”

“I’ll keep an eye out.”

Jane bit into her jelly biscuit and munched on the sticky sweetness while attempting to shrug off Robert’s teasing. Being thirty-five and never married did make her wonder if there was a Mr. Right for her. Especially since there would be two Mr. Wrongs in attendance this weekend. Singleness had its advantages. Not answering to anyone about where you were going. Not having to explain your purchases and listen to someone criticize your color choices. But sometimes she thought it would be nice to have someone who cared where she was going, or to enjoy purchases with, or to help decide color choices.

Robert had agreed to be her non-boyfriend employer and weekend guest, who everyone would assume was really her boyfriend covered in the cloak of professionalism.

But in truth, when teetering on the brink of romance during their last big case, they'd agreed he was her boss and there would be no personal attachments. So, for Jane, the 'always a bridesmaid never a bride' may hold true.

Finishing her biscuit, she wiped her hands and held them up. "No sticky." Robert nodded and Jane reached for the three-ring binder containing the Singletary murder investigation and laid it on her lap.

She had enjoyed the mental exercise of delving into investigation assignments with Robert, but this was the first case she had examined where she knew the people involved.

Now to find something that might move suspicion from Mr. Sing ... or was she guilty of entering the case with preconceived notions too? She pulled out her rule list. Yup, #4. Resist the urge to become personally involved with potential witnesses. But she couldn't change the past. She was personally involved. Like it or not, her view was biased. Robert had to be wrong about Mr. Singletary.

~

Driving Jane's car, Robert merged into interstate traffic bound for Eaglemont. He'd have taken his truck, but Jane insisted on taking her car because it was her event, would take less gas, and save wear and tear on his truck. But in the Honda hatchback, he'd have to get used to being close to the road and looking up to other vehicles.

"First question," Jane said, tapping the binder cover. "Why is the case called cold?"

"When leads in a criminal investigation stop being actively pursued because of lack of evidence, the trail has run cold. But a cold case remains open, pending the discovery of new evidence."

"Is a case initially considered hot?"

"I've never heard the term 'hot' for a case, just active. Although hot is an accurate way to think of it—hot on the trail." Robert pulled past a semi and tightened his hands on the wheel. "I'm used to riding higher with the big dogs. In your car, I'm a little Yorkie."

"Yorkies are adorable. You'll get the feel of it. I'm having to make a leap too, shifting from wedding traditions to murder. Where do I start?"

"Read the synopsis and crime scene description, then the statements. You'll notice I interviewed your friend, Phillip Randolph, about the four hundred dollars missing from the Singletary house."

"Do you think he'll remember you?"

"We'll see." He ran his hand over his scratchy whiskers. "I didn't have a beard then. Just read and see what stands out to you. I'd like your take on the case, and what you remember of the circumstances and people during the time of the murder."

She creased her brows and nodded.

He and Jane had developed a natural flow in case analysis, piggy backing off each other's ideas to get at the truth. But would it work in this case?

Robert set the cruise control and settled back. A wedding might be a rite of passage and so was death, but not murder. Murder was undeserved death and required justice.

Reviewing the murder returned him to the Singletary crime scene.

Robert hadn't been with the Alabama Bureau of Investigation (ABI) for very long. He'd just settled down with a bowl of popcorn and a Coke for a late-night viewing of his recording of the season finale of *JAG*. The script provided prime time entertainment where the bad guys were caught and punished. Every week the Navy's Office of the Judge Advocate General managed to handle a criminal case with all its complications in one hour.

His division head called at 11:00 p.m. regarding the murder in Valleytown. Three hours later, his headlights reflected the 705 on the mailbox in front of the brick one-story home on Wren Drive. He pulled in behind the sheriff's car and state crime scene van. Yellow tape surrounded the perimeter of the yard and cordoned off curious onlookers who had ventured out at the early morning hour. Inside, crime scene investigators gathered physical evidence, dusted for fingerprints, and took photos and video of the scene.

His job was to conduct interviews and pull clues together to find out what happened. And possibly discern who murdered Veronica Singletary.

The deceased lay face up on the gray tile kitchen floor surrounded by an overturned basket and several scattered peaches. Her head was wedged against the leg of the kitchen table. A cut on her forehead had bled and showed bruising. The telltale blood stain on her blouse gave evidence to a gunshot. According to initial inquiries, Martin discovered his wife's body at 9:45 p.m.

The writers of *JAG* would have resolved the Singletary murder in an hour. Eighteen years later and the murder remained unsolved. No bad guy apprehended. No one punished. This unfinished business left a blot on his perfect solve record.

"This is so sad," Jane said, looking up from her reading. "Poor Mr. Singletary walking in and finding his wife dead on the kitchen floor. It's awful to think the gun he gave her for protection killed her."

Robert stared at the road ahead. "I have a problem with his statement about the gun. He says he purchased it after the other break-ins in the neighborhood. But the break-ins were in May, and he purchased the gun in April."

"Yes, but Mr. Singletary said in his statement, 'Due to rehearsals, I'm gone at night, so I got her a gun to allay her fears,' which sounds like her being uncomfortable alone may have come up before the neighborhood break-ins, and he just forgot the sequence."

"Okay, but there were other inconsistencies."

"Like what?"

"Mr. Singletary mentioned the missing four hundred dollars he supposedly withdrew for a choir camp, but the camp was two months away. Then he claimed students in his class heard him discussing the money with his wife, who had stopped by the school. But he didn't have a class at the time; it was his planning period."

"There is a logical explanation for him to refer to his class overhearing the discussion with his wife because he let the ensemble students eat lunch in the choir room during his planning period. I'd have probably been there, except my 4th period class had first lunch."

"He spoke of senior boys wanting money for a trip to Europe and claimed he hated mentioning one of the students had been in trouble for stealing. For someone who asserted that he didn't like to cast suspicion, he did it with very little hesitation."

"He was probably referring to Phillip being in trouble for stealing, which was true. He had to complete community service hours."

Jane was coming up with plausible explanations, but Singletary's stating suspicions bothered him. He pressed too hard to tie the burglary to the murder while claiming to hate offering solutions. "Deflecting guilt, offering solutions, and placing blame are textbook liar responses."

"Textbook? Are you jumping to conclusions based on circumstantial evidence and prejudging? What happened to everyone is a suspect until they are not a suspect?"

Sucker punch to the chest. He'd taught Jane well, and she wasn't finished.

"As for Mr. Sing giving reasons behind the murder, that was characteristic of him. If we had a problem in choir—maybe not getting a pitch right—he'd suggest reasons and help us get past the snag. It is not surprising he would offer solutions to his wife's death," Jane let out a heavy sigh, "although if I were in his shoes, I doubt I could think straight."

Jane's analysis was stinging him like a shot from a BB gun. He had to admit he'd placed his focus on Martin Singletary from the start, and Jane was giving him plenty of fodder for re-examining the case without prejudice.

"Chilton County peaches ahead," Jane pointed to a sign.

Saved by a billboard. "Perfect, and there is a drive-thru."

They made a quick stop, and Jane resumed reading. Soon, a sweet peach aroma filled his senses. "It's ironic. This case occurred during peach season, and we are reviewing it at the same time of year. When I arrived at the murder scene, a basket of peaches had spilled and were scattered on the floor."

"I read a rhinestone and broken fingernail were found in smashed peaches beneath the victim," Jane said. "I understand your qualms about the case. And I admit it's hard for me to be objective. My subjective mind doesn't want Mr. Sing to be the murderer. It just seems the partial footprint found in the dirt next to the forced entry at the rear door, points to an interrupted burglary and struggle over the gun. And above all the concerns you have, Mr. Singletary has an alibi. I was with him along with about three hundred others at a high school concert at the time of the murder."

"I know. I interviewed the principal and talked to the secretary at your high school."

"And?"

"The principal confirmed Mr. Singletary and the choir were present at the tri-county high school event. But Ms. Finderbush also shared that Veronica Singletary had come back by the office and inquired about the date of the summer camp. Which tells me Veronica doubted the choir retreat was the reason for Martin Singletary's cash withdrawal."

Jane raised a brow. "Ms. Finderbush always had her finger on the pulse of school activity."

"She also informed me, when I called to get the location of the tri-county event while preparing my final report, that Mr. Singletary had already remarried and had a baby on the way."

"Mr. Sing married the drama teacher who handled

show choir choreography. Why did Ms. Finderbush bring up Mr. Sing's marriage?"

Robert attempted to mimic the secretary. "With all the shows the choir attends, Martin marrying the drama teacher at the end of July," he poked his index finger in the air, "—with a baby on the way too—is cheaper. The school system pays for one instead of two instructor rooms when the choir goes out of town."

Jane laughed. "You make a perfect double for Ms. Finderbush."

"Maybe, but your Mr. Sing wouldn't be a good double to play Richard Kimble in heavy pursuit of his wife's murderer on *The Fugitive*."

"People react to tragedy in different ways."

Robert shrugged. Was he the only one who saw Martin Singletary's quick remarriage as a motive for murder?

"Whatever the truth behind the murder," Jane said, "it resulted in Veronica's last peach season. She was only twenty-four years old. It's so unfair."

"I agree." The peach smell in the car had become intoxicating. "And the tragic loss of life is the reason the case still worries me."

Jane closed the murder case file. "So, are we good now? Your misgivings with Mr. Singletary all have logical explanations, don't you think?"

Even though something at his gut level told him differently, he also knew he could have been more thorough in his investigation. With help from Vance,

Robert had already requested the crime scene evidence at the murder scene as well as at the neighborhood burglaries be analyzed using new forensic techniques. He would wait and see if new clues emerged. For the sake of not messing up Jane's plans for now, he would shelve his suspicions, hope that his past association with the case would go unrecognized, and he'd play the role of Jane's friendly non-boyfriend employer.

CHAPTER FOUR

The Eaglemont name carved in stone on a pillar of natural rock marked the entrance to the lodge on Mountain Air Circle.

"Here we are at Alabama's side of Lookout Mountain," Jane said with excitement.

Robert shifted to a lower gear, turning onto the uphill disappearing drive bordered by thick woods. "I'm ready for my history lesson."

Jane placed the murder book on the floorboard and pulled the large packet from her purse with lodge instructions and history. Ready to trade cold case thoughts for the wonders of nature and fresh forest smells, she rolled down her window. "This section of Lookout Mountain is at the tail-end of the Cumberland Plateau and the mountain stretches into parts of Georgia and Tennessee."

"Different terrain from lower Alabama," Robert said.

"I can already tell it's cooler." Black-eyed Susans of gold and black grew wild along the sloping shoulders of the road. "These flowers will be perfect for the craft activity I have planned. Rosemary and Phillip's wedding deserves to be magical."

"With your planning, I'm sure the event will be perfect."

"Thank you for the vote of confidence."

"How did you and Rosemary become such close friends?"

"We formed a club in sixth grade." Jane slid into the memory.

It was chilly, and she'd snuggled deep into the warm flannel lining of her sleeping bag. "Rosemary, Cecelia and I were camping behind my grandmother's house. We saw a shooting star streak the sky. Rosemary said it was a lucky sign and the Shooting Stars Club was born. Our club song is "Stars Fell on Alabama". We have a motto and everything."

Robert glanced at her and grinned. "Cute. I remember when I first heard about the song. It's funny to think of all the memories the night sky spawns. I was camping with my dad in Pine Bluff. With very little moonlight, the stars stood out against the dark black sky, and we saw a succession of shooting stars."

"A meteor shower?"

"Yes. He told me about the song. My dad said he proposed to my mom under a starlit sky."

"Sounds romantic. I'd love to see a meteor shower."

"It's a spectacular sight. Dad said the streak is not really a star but meteor particles entering earth's atmosphere at such high speed they create fireballs we call shooting stars."

Jane chuckled. "A fireball could describe Rosemary. Wait till you meet her. My grandma called her a spitfire. As Shooting Stars, we pledged to be at each other's weddings. Cecelia and Arnold jumped ahead of Rosemary and me and eloped right before graduation. But we threw a festive reception for them. Naturally, Rosemary's event has to be memorable."

The end of the forested drive yielded to a manicured lawn and circular drive. The stark contrast paralleled Jane's emotions of excitement over Rosemary's wedding and her anxiety, not only about the murder case, but about asking Robert to be her non-boyfriend date. She had put him on the spot, asking him to come. He'd agreed, but what else could he do? She'd pushed to get their cases caught up and he was a man of his word.

Continuing along the drive, Eaglemont lodge came into view.

Robert stopped the car. "Wow. Look at this place."

The two-story lodge was a proud display of natural stone and boasted a steep gabled roof outlined with cedar timbers. Jane had committed the layout of the property to memory. "Drive around the side. There is a kitchen entry where we can offload the food first."

Robert drove to the side of the lodge, opened the hatchback, and removed the cooler and grocery bags. "You said the owners gave this estate to the county?"

"Eaglemont was built in the 1930s by Harlan King who owned the King Eagle grocery chain. He passed away in 1972 and bequeathed the lodge to the local historical society."

Robert nodded toward the outside of the building. "The stone construction appears to be hand hewn."

She touched the rough edges of the rock exterior made of varied shapes and tones of grays and brown. "This stone was quarried in the area and stone masons individually fit every piece together."

Robert craned his neck. "The lodge is a massive 3-D puzzle. The perfect place to fit together clues to solve a murder."

"If you're trying to rattle me, you're succeeding."

"Don't worry. I didn't bring a bare light bulb to hang over your friends' heads for questioning." He cut his eyes in her direction. "I shall be the beacon of discretion."

She didn't doubt Robert's integrity, but the possibility of the old murder case coming to light admittedly left her uneasy.

However, when he met the ensemble group and heard how Mr. Sing took extra time with his students to develop their talents, Robert would be impressed and change his mind about their music teacher. Mr. Sing was no murderer. And if Mr. Singletary did come,

Robert would observe his charisma at work. *Relax, Jane*. She took a deep breath, inhaling the mountain air.

"Remember, table those murder thoughts. Happy wedding thoughts please."

"Yes, ma'am."

Jane pulled the cooler on wheels, and Robert followed with the food bags.

"Look at this inscription by the kitchen door," Robert said. "Without labor, nothing prospers — Sophocles. True words."

"Be on the lookout for quotes and words of wisdom inscribed in stone throughout the property."

The code numbers beeped as Jane entered them in the keyless door lock. She opened the door and stepped onto the service porch, leading to the kitchen.

"There's a refrigerator out here. This service porch will serve as our sanitation area for extra safety when people arrive. Everything I brought has been cleaned with sanitation wipes." And she hoped the cleansing extended to the fresh point of view Robert promised regarding the murder case.

~

After offloading food items, Robert backed out of the service drive and parked under the front portico. Opening the hatchback, he maneuvered the trunk out, lowering the heavy load to pavement, then helped Jane unload their smaller bags. Jane towed her suitcase on rollers with Robert's smaller duffel bag stacked on top, while Robert lugged the trunk.

Etched in the stone beside the massive double wooden front doors was: *Eaglemont—for Relaxation and Renewal.*

"I'm glad to see that quote," Robert said. "I'll need R and R after carrying this trunk."

"You won't have to carry it much farther." Jane punched the code into the number-lock entry. Inside, the foyer alone was as large as his living room. Robert lowered the trunk with a grunt to the stone paved flooring and the clunk echoed throughout the expansive space.

The huge meeting hall to the right of the entry had open beamed rafters, a wagon wheel chandelier, polished red oak floors, with rich leather and wood furniture, rustic accessories, and an imposing stone fireplace at the end of the room.

Robert whistled. "The palace ballroom we twirled around in the Caribbean could fit inside here."

"I think you're right. The floor plan lists the activity room as sixty by thirty feet."

"Where to with this trunk?"

"Since your room is downstairs, are you okay with me storing the trunk with you?"

"Why not take the room next to mine and keep the trunk with you?"

"My room is upstairs. We don't want them thinking ... you know ... with the rooms so close—"

"And they won't think I can climb stairs?"

"Unless married, I've planned for guys downstairs

and girls up, in separate rooms."

Robert hiked a brow. "I get it. You want to keep them guessing about our relationship. We couldn't very well do that rooming next to each other. So separated we shall be, presenting decorum that you really want to have them interpret as a cover-up. Yet our cover-up is false, and the illusion is true. Oh, what a tangled web we weave. I don't know who said it," he made a sweeping motion, "but it's worthy to go on a wall in this place."

"Mr. Grey, the astute."

"No. I think it's Mr. Grey the porter, feels like you packed rocks."

"It's filled with wedding things."

"What wedding things weigh so much?"

"Welcome bags and items for wedding activities, but it's probably my mother's dishes and pots and pans for Rosemary that make it so heavy."

"You think? At least the groom gets to haul it off," he muttered. "Where's my room?"

"To the left. Let me take hold of one end of the trunk and help you."

"No. I have it balanced. You bring the luggage and lead the way."

Jane moved to the left of the foyer, through a cozy sitting room with a small fireplace and on to a hallway on the other side. "All the bedrooms are in this wing."

She opened the door to room 101. "Here's your room. Set the trunk just inside the door. Duffle bag on your bed, okay?"

"Suits me." Robert hefted the trunk through the door and set it down with a groan. Then he plunked down on the edge of the bed, shaking his arms.

"Are you all right?"

"Just trying to get the feeling back."

Jane clasped her hands in adoring fashion. "You're my superhero."

"If I were a superhero, my arms wouldn't feel like stretched out rubber bands."

Jane flipped open the latches on the trunk. "Your reward. You'll be the first to receive a wedding welcome bag." She held up a bright yellow bag with ribbons of red, orange, and hot pink tied to the handles. "Sunrise colors. Welcome to Eaglemont."

"Any food in the bag? I'm famished after my hauling labor."

"I included favorite snacks of the bride and groom." Jane tossed him the bag and removed the others from the trunk.

"Peanuts. Phillip has good taste." Robert opened the pack and savored the crunchy goodness while rustling through the other contents. "Is this the choir?" He held up a photo. "Kind of a small choir."

"It's a picture of the ensemble. We were part of the regular choir."

"Weren't you cute with the bow in your hair."

Jane sat beside Robert. "Those were our Gershwin show tune costumes. Next to me is Cecelia, we both sang soprano." She slid her finger across the photo. "Rosemary, alto."

"Let me guess. This big guy was one of your boyfriends?"

"Nope. That's Phillip, the groom. He sang bass."

Robert took a closer look. "Yes, I remember him now."

"There's Evan Armstrong, who is now my assistant principal. He sang tenor." What did Jane ever see in him? The guy was scrawny and had brown shaggy hair shading his eyes.

"Next is Darin, our baritone."

Darin was different. He had blond, curly hair cut short. He was muscular and had a smile a sourpuss couldn't resist. "Ah. Rival boyfriends stood together?"

Jane jarred him with a shoulder punch. "I mostly dated Evan and in high school and Darin in college. The six of us together formed the Valley Voices."

"I recognize Singletary, standing to the side. He doesn't look much older than you students."

"He was twenty-three, only five years older."

Robert pursed his lips. "You indicated he was loved and admired by the students. Why?"

"Well ... he was like one of us. He kidded with us, always had time for us, and spent extra hours developing our show choir techniques. The drama teacher, who is now Mrs. Singletary, choreographed our shows. We put on a good performance."

"And the only thing you were better at was

humility?"

"Funny. You'll see." She reached back into the trunk. "I brought proof." She held up a DVD.

Robert winced. "I bet you want us to all gather around and watch."

"Of course. One of the evening activities I planned as—"

"—maid of honor. I thought all the maid of honor did was stand next to the bride and hold her bouquet during the ceremony, and maybe straighten the dress if it had a long train."

"If she is conscientious, the maid of honor has way more responsibilities. She handles the music playlist for the reception, helps plan food, flowers, and activities for the wedding weekend, presents a toast to the couple at the reception, keeps an eye on the groom so he doesn't cross paths with the bride on the wedding day, plans the bachelorette party and makes welcome bags for overnight wedding guests." She paused and drew in a breath.

Robert pulled a honey bun from the bag. "The bride has excellent taste in her maid of honor selection and favorite snack. Any chance of a cup of coffee to go with this?"

Jane dangled welcome bags in front of his nose. "If you help place these welcome bags." She handed him four.

"I feel like a dog begging for a bone."

Robert listened to Jane's instructions. "Place a bag in

rooms 103 and 106 for Phillip and Evan. Darin is married and will have the double room 105. Put two bags there. Room 102, across from you, is another double in case Mr. Singletary and his wife come. I'll reserve bags for them."

"Wait. Shouldn't Phillip have a double? He's the one getting married."

"Rosemary has the honeymoon suite upstairs. Phillip can join her after the wedding. Actually, the lodge is rented for a week. When the rest of us leave Saturday, Rosemary and Phil can use any bedroom they want."

"Big place for two people who won't be social distancing." He winked.

"Who knows? Everyone needs space on occasion." Jane smirked and grabbed a carton of Yoo-hoo drinks from the trunk. "A treat for Rosemary's suite. I'll distribute welcome bags upstairs and meet you down here to make coffee."

"Yes, MH."

"MH?"

"Maid of Honor."

She grinned and left him.

They had only eaten apple slices, potato chips, and water on the trip to the lodge. He funneled the remaining peanuts into his mouth and munched the salty nuggets.

The room sparked remembrances from his hometown. Running his hand over the soft white chenille bedspread on the simple black iron bedstead reminded him of lying next to his grandma as she read to him. The bathroom had a pedestal sink and black and white one-inch vintage tile like the floor in the downtown Pine Bluff drug store.

He made quick work of his welcome bag assignment, making drops in the other homespun rooms, and returned to the sitting room to wait for Jane. The staircase to the second floor was made of peeled log sections cut in half and sanded smooth to form steps inside the stone stairwell. Etched in stone at the foot of the stairs was another inscription: *Be not simply good, be good for something, Thoreau.* An etching to motivate or possibly enhance an inferiority complex.

Jane came down the stairs. "The sayings carved all around are interesting. At the top of the stairs is Emerson's happy reminder that the sun will shine after every storm."

"If walls could talk, these would really have something to say."

"Profound, Mr. Detective." Jane tilted her head toward the kitchen. "Ready to make coffee?"

In the farmhouse style kitchen, nostalgia struck again. "This lodge is bringing back growing up memories in Pine Bluff." He patted the deep white porcelain sink. "I used to stand beside a sink like this in grandma's kitchen waiting to lick the bowl when she stirred up a pound cake."

Jane paused and stared at the sink for a moment, then smiled. "You are fortunate to have grown up with your family intact." She pointed at the countertop. "I don't see a coffeemaker. Help me search the cabinets."

The cupboards had glass-fronted, open shelving. Robert pulled back the brown checked fabric from under the sink. Among the ceramic bowls, cast-iron and aluminum pans was an old-fashioned stove top percolator.

He grabbed the handle and held it up. "Know how to use one of these?"

"No. Do you?"

"I'm willing to learn."

He removed the lid with a glass knob on top. Inside, he lifted out the basket with holes fitted over a stem.

Jane looked it over. "My grandmother had one like this, but she put sunflowers in it and used it for a centerpiece. She made coffee in an electric drip coffee maker."

"My dad used one similar to this when we camped. The coffee probably goes in the basket."

Jane held up the pot and giggled. "We've become teens on YouTube not knowing how to operate a rotary dial telephone."

"Maybe someone posted how to make coffee with this thing."

After following instructions on a phone video, the coffee pot gurgled, brown-colored water bobbed up and down in the glass top on the lid, and coffee aroma filled the kitchen.

Jane's phone sounded.

Robert watched the bubbling brew while Jane issued instructions to come to the side entrance.

"Rosemary and Phillip are ten minutes away and Evan is right behind her."

Just enough time for him to devour his honey bun welcome treat and coffee before peace and quiet disappeared.

When Rosemary Greene entered the kitchen, she was a presence not to be ignored. She had lots of red fluffed hair and wide, red, cat eyeglasses. She blinked at him with magnified green eyes when introductions were made then grabbed him in a hefty hug.

"I'm honored to meet you and have you at my wedding."

She linked arms with Jane and spoke with a raspy voice. "It's going to be so great to have the old gang together. And not just together but quarantined together. Something akin to blood brothers, don't you think?"

She elbowed Phillip, a solid built fellow with a military buzz haircut. He looked every bit the Special Ops guy he was. He lifted his shoulders and his stern face melted to a soft countenance. "Not sure, babe."

A high-pitched voice coming from the service porch commented, "Here's hoping all the safety measures we've taken keep us protected from the 'evil Corona', as the kids at school say."

A couple strolled in. Robert recognized Evan Armstrong from the ensemble photo. He was the man who had pestered Jane about returning to teaching before her leave time was over. With his arm wrapped around the waist of the girl with him, he presented her to the group. "Everyone, this is Caroline Warner. Meet Rosemary and Phillip, the couple stepping into wedded bliss and Jane, whose place you took in the kindergarten."

The girl, probably early twenties, smiled and nodded.

He turned to Robert. "And you are?"

"What Jane brought with her."

Jane jumped in. "This is Robert Grey, the man I work for."

"Ah ... the private investigator." His eyes moved over Robert. "Well, who would have thought our Jane from Valley Voices would end up working for an investigator."

Evan turned back to Jane. "I was lucky to find Caroline midyear when I couldn't convince you to come back. Like you, she went to the University of Alabama. She just finished her master's in elementary education, *and* she was a Capstone Woman at the university."

"Roll Tide." Jane offered her a high five and Caroline let out a soft, feminine giggle.

"Since you stayed out the full school year, Caroline will return in the kindergarten slot. You're more experienced, so I've lined you up for fifth grade next year. Of course, with the pandemic, there will be different avenues of instruction—online classes and the like. I was not able to hold the kindergarten position for you. Can't say I didn't warn you." Evan jiggled his index finger at Jane as if she'd been a naughty girl. "But I'm guessing playing private eye was worth it?"

Jane flinched, then took a step back and stiffened.

Robert felt steam rising inside. What a jerk. "She doesn't play. Jane carries a badge."

"Oh?" Evan's eyes rolled over Jane, scrutinizing her in the same way he had Robert. "Well, good for you."

"How exciting." Caroline clasped her hands together. "You must show us your badge."

Rosemary cut in. "I don't need to see a badge to know I'm fortunate to have this multi-talented woman, who doesn't get near the appreciation she deserves," she sent Evan a dagger-laced stare, "as my maid of honor. Coffee smells good. Any more?"

Jane's grandma was right, Rosemary was a spitfire. Jane recovered. "Sure. We just made a full pot."

"Good." She grabbed Phillip's arm. "Give us instructions on where to offload our bags and we'll sit down for a cup."

"Leave your food items on the service porch," Jane instructed. "There is a refrigerator for cold items out there. We can wipe items down and bring them in and organize later. Drive around front and bring your luggage into the lobby."

Rosemary and Phillip left.

Evan handed Caroline a bottle of sparkling Perrier

mineral water. "Stay here and help Jane with the food. I'll take care of the luggage."

"You're really a detective?" Caroline asked Jane. "It's great to meet finally. I've heard so much about you from the school staff."

Robert rumpled his honey bun wrapper and tossed it in the trash, then rinsed his coffee cup. Caroline seemed sweet but clueless as to the animosity and hurt feelings Evan had stirred. And he did it with a smile. Robert would have liked to erase the smirk from his face, like marker off whiteboard.

Jane went to the service porch and picked up one of the grocery bags. "Bring in the other bag," Jane instructed Caroline. "These items are cleaned. You can help me organize. Robert, could you open the front door? We'll join you as soon as we put things away."

"Sure. No problem." But he did have a problem with Evan. How did Jane do it? He couldn't be so accepting of the girl who stole her job.

Robert cut through the vast expanse of the great room. The open rafters and mountain view should have evoked a restful ambiance, but inside irritation festered. He didn't know how Jane felt about fifth grade, but she looked shocked by the move. What kind of principal announces to his teacher on compassionate leave of absence that she has been permanently replaced—in front of the teacher who took her place and her good friends? He put Jane and even Caroline in a terrible spot. He had no use for him but would tolerate him for the time being.

He made his way to the foyer, fixed a smile on his face, and opened the front door. At the sight of the lodge's interior, Rosemary let out high-pitched cackle. Curiously, her hair matched the color of the cedar rafters.

Robert helped with the unloading process. Evan was a combination of scammer and opportunist. He had bugged Jane and played on her vulnerabilities, saying she could lose her insurance and retirement benefits. But Jane had told him the real reason he wanted her back. Her tenured service would boost his credentials as an administrator. He wanted her for self-gain.

He let the last bag with Evan's name tag on it drop heavily on the stone foyer floor. Maybe there was something breakable inside. He tamped down a twinge of guilt when Rosemary read aloud the inscription inside the entry.

May the grace of God's protection
And his great love abide,
Within the home and the hearts of
All who dwell inside.

So far, the dwellers in this place included a cackling bride, a tough Air Force Special Ops man, a naive teacher, and a pompous cad.

Robert sucked in air and prayed God's will and wisdom would replace any unpleasant thoughts about those he would be dwelling with for the next few days.

CHAPTER FIVE

Jane sorted canned goods while Caroline found a shelf for the boxed items. Eleven years of service and she was being replaced by one who's been teaching five months? She was Evan's old mama dog who must take a back seat to the cute new pup. Jane swallowed hard against the pain in her throat.

No wonder Evan quit bugging her about returning early. Jane might have experience, but Caroline had a master's degree—a likely plus for Evan's climb up the administrative ladder. Being a Capstone Woman at the University of Alabama meant she had congeniality skills as a part of an elite group who assisted the University president's office, admissions, and alumni during functions held on campus.

At least Caroline had gotten Evan off her back—way off, but off. She couldn't blame him for moving ahead with his ultimate quest for a principal's job, but did he have to sacrifice her along the way? *Get it together, Jane*. She was here for Rosemary and Phillip.

Finished in the kitchen, Caroline and Jane joined Rosemary, enjoying the mountain view from the great room. But the distant haze shrouding the mountain range, mixed with the slight musky odor from the fireplace and the heavy smell of lemon scented furniture polish added weight to the discouragement settling on Jane's shoulders.

She hadn't been looking forward to going back to teaching but was at least well-versed in the kindergarten curriculum and had developed techniques that worked with the students. But fifth grade? She'd heard the groans in the teacher's lounge from the fifth-grade teachers about the attitudes encountered in the higher grade: "They think they know it all, talk back, and refuse to work," and "I had one threaten me with a lawsuit for giving his shoulder a shake to wake him up."

An involuntary shiver traveled down her spine. Teaching kindergarten students wasn't always pleasant, but five-year-olds were sweet, ready to learn, wanted to please, and looked up to their teachers.

Was she destined to be relegated to the second-rate, 'always the bridesmaid, never the bride' league? Her father left her and her brother, whom she'd adored, went with him. Darin had dropped her for a better deal, and now Evan had cast her aside.

Too many negative thoughts. She shook her head and hugged her arms to her middle, burying her discontent. With Evan's unexpected announcement, she'd better steel herself against the appearance of Darin with his socialite wife.

Rosemary snapped her fingers in front of her face and peered over her red-rimmed glasses. "Jane. You with us? Where do we take the luggage?"

"Sorry." Jane needed to remember what and who she was there for. She returned to the foyer, where Phillip and Robert waited.

Evan came in the open door, carrying an armload of small bags. "Look what the cat dragged in."

"Cecelia. Arnold. Yay!" Rosemary grabbed Cecelia in a hug.

"The cat who dragged me in was Cecelia," Arnold said, laden with luggage, "but I'm glad she did."

"Can you believe it?" Evan said. "I live in Valleytown with Rosemary, Cecelia and Arnold and we have to climb a mountain to see each other."

"With the pandemic, we don't leave the house very often but working from home has given us lots of family togetherness." Cecelia smiled and patted Arnold's shoulder.

"So together, we had to stay on our twelve-year-old son's back about completing online school assignments," Arnold said. "Thank goodness for summer break and grandparents to take him in so we could be here."

"What about Amy? How old is she now?" Jane asked.

"Amy is seventeen and at a music camp. She had to go through the same pandemic preparations as we did."

"How about chitchat later. I'd like to get these bags deposited," Evan said. "Where's Caroline's room?"

"Ladies upstairs, except for Arnold. You're upstairs with Cecelia," Jane said. "Guys, your rooms are downstairs. Men, follow me with the ladies' bags." Jane led them through the sitting room to the log staircase where she stepped aside and motioned to Rosemary, Cecelia, and Caroline to go ahead of her. "Cecelia, room 202, Caroline 203, and Rosemary, you're in the suite at the end of the hall."

"Arnold, be sure to get the gun from the console in the car," Cecelia called down to her husband.

"You've got a handgun permit?" Evan asked.

"I do." Arnold said. "Best practice these days."

Evan whacked Arnold on the shoulder. "I can rest easier in Valleytown now, knowing you have a gun."

Evan's joking remarks were encroaching on Jane's already roughed up nerve endings. Left in the trail of Caroline's perfume, Jane climbed the stairs, with Robert right behind her.

At the top of the stairs, Jane latched onto Emerson's idea of the sun shining after every storm. Eagles could fly high above the storms. At Eaglemont, she would have to do the same. Jane pointed to the quote and spoke so all could hear. "Everyone, there are encouraging quotes etched in stone all around the property. You will want to keep an eye out for them."

Outside room 203, Caroline took the two smaller bags of the four Evan cradled in one arm. His other hand grasped the handle of a roller bag.

Hands on hips, Rosemary said, "How long were you planning on staying?"

Caroline hooked a strand of highlighted hair behind her ear and smiled sweetly. "I always over-pack. Be prepared is my motto."

"I thought that was the Boy Scout motto," Robert whispered in Jane's ear. He had carried one of Arnold's bags upstairs.

She grinned. His levity diminished her envy. Jane motioned to the room catty-corner from Caroline's. "Cecelia and Arnold, here's your room."

"Arnold, you know we'll have to kick you out before the bachelorette party Friday night," Rosemary teased, making her way to the end of the hall.

"No sweat. I'll be busy with what we've cooked up for Phillip downstairs."

Jane caught up with Rosemary. "We'll use your suite for the bachelorette party, then it can become the honeymoon suite after the wedding."

"When the rest of you can skedaddle and leave me with my man from Afghanistan," she said and reached to squeeze Phillip's chin and winked at him through her signature colorful glasses with the upturned corners.

"I'm with you, babe," Phillip said, keeping a straight

face.

"Can we take a peek in your suite now?" Caroline asked.

"Why not? Phil, bring my bags in. Jane, give everyone the three-dollar tour since you know all the particulars."

Jane narrated. "The suite is complete with a platform king size bed overlooking the very beginning of the Appalachian Mountains. There is a hot tub on the balcony, and a bathroom complete with a walk-in shower and jacuzzi. And … a sitting room with a small kitchen stocked with Yoo-hoo drinks and fireballs."

Rosemary let out a "Yoo-hoo!" Everyone laughed. "Our standard snack on high school bus trips."

"Yes, and Rosemary kept everyone in stitches with her antics, just as she does now," Cecelia said.

"She had to act pretty crazy sitting next to tight-lipped Phil," Evan said. "Am I right old buddy?"

Phillip returned a shoulder shrug.

"Evan is right." Rosemary squeezed Phillip's cheeks between her thumb and index finger. "He takes a bit of coaxing. But wow … when I get those dimples to pop … it's time to sing the Hallelujah Chorus."

The doorbell rang.

The Valleytown contingent froze.

"Something wrong?" Robert asked.

"The doorbell plays 'Climb Every Mountain'—one of the songs the ensemble performed," Evan said.

"I'll get the door," Jane said. "It should be Darin and

his wife. Robert, please show the men their rooms."

Jane tugged open the thick lodge door and was taken back with the impact of the cobalt eyes and the soft smile of Darin Foster. He stood there in khaki slacks with a pale blue button-down shirt, making his eyes appear bluer. He'd added a clean-cut beard and mustache since she had seen him last. He had likely grown accustomed to using a stylist in the circles he was involved in with his trend-setter wife.

His gaze covered her with an eerie throwback feeling. "Was that our song?"

"What?" They never had a song when they dated.

"The doorbell. One of our ensemble songs."

"Oh. Yes. An interesting coincidence but appropriate for a mountain top lodge. Rosemary used to give me chills singing the solo."

"Standing next to you gave me chills."

Was he flirting? Where was his wife? "Don't talk about chills in a pandemic."

"Hey. I'm officially Covid free and did my fourteen days of quarantine. Here's my certificate." He held up a paper. "Do I get a hug?"

"Absolutely." Jane reached up and hugged him, his beard tickling her cheek. "Where's Cynthia?"

His mouth upturned in one corner. "You haven't heard?" Then he shook his head. "No reason you should. I haven't broadcast it. Cynthia and I are divorced. Final in October."

"Sorry I ... had no idea."

"Okay if I come in?"

She shook off the news. "Of course. Everyone just arrived. Gather all your stuff and I can show you to your room. It's exciting to have the old group together."

He held up a small bag suitable for an airline carryon. "This is all I brought."

She motioned him in. "Follow me."

The men had converged in the sitting room, where they greeted Darin. Robert wrinkled his brow and stepped aside, looking every bit the outsider he was. The look on his face told Jane the sacrifice he was enduring. She'd have to make him feel more comfortable.

"Darin, I'd like you to meet Robert Grey, my boss."

Darin extended his hand, presenting his winsome grin. "Pleased to meet you."

"He's a private investigator," Evan said.

When Arnold and Phillip drew into the conversation, Darin touched Jane's elbow and pulled her aside.

"We have a lot of catching up to do. I hope you'll reserve some time for me."

"Sure. But we'll all be catching up." This is the guy who dumped her for Cynthia. Now he had singled her out and wanted to catch up? If she were butter, she'd have turned into a puddle at his feet, and she hated herself for it.

~

Robert was invisible, which was fine with him. He stood just outside the men's circle. He'd rather observe and listen than socialize. Giddy girl laughter filtered down from upstairs.

"I'm going to check on the girls while you guys talk," Jane said.

Robert had promised Jane discretion in regard to the cold case, but he would like to discover covertly more about each of these men who might be able to shed light on what happened the night Veronica Singletary died.

Phillip fascinated him. His eyebrows came to a pointed arch over dark, almost black eyes. He was muscled and lean and looked like a guy trained to thrust a knife in your belly, if the situation warranted it.

"Phil," Darin said, "like the tortoise and the hare you took your time, but you win the prize getting Rosemary at long last."

Evan and Arnold nodded.

"And this observation comes from a bunch of hares," Phillip said, crossing his arms.

"You're right," Evan said, his hand swept around the group. Since Robert was invisible the hand sweep didn't include him. "Every one of us made quick attachments. Arnold here first out of the gate, surprising us all. Then I guess it was me with my less-than-a-year try at marital bliss. Darin here tells us he just joined the ranks of divorcee."

"Hear, hear. There can be bliss in divorce as well as weddings." Darin wiggled his brows, bringing laughter to the circle.

"I thought the spotlight was supposed to be on Phillip and Rosemary," Arnold said.

"Good point coming from the man with the spotlight." Darin briskly rubbed his hands together. "You were always good with the technical end of things."

"Without a stellar voice, handling the sound and lights was my way to stay close to Cecelia."

"Your technical skill has paid off," Evan said. "Arnold's IT business in Valleytown keeps all our electronics running in the school system. Darin, bring your accounting skills to Valleytown. The school board is looking for someone."

"For now, I'm sticking with financial advising." Darin shifted the job question to Phil. "What will your responsibilities be stateside?"

"To finish my twenty, I'll be a PME instructor—Professional Military Education, training enlisted men at Maxwell Air Force Base."

Darin, who stood as tall as Phil's six feet plus, draped his arm around Phil's shoulder. "You're going to be in training too, buddy—taming Rosemary."

Evan slapped his leg and snorted. "A harder task than Special Ops."

Phillip raised a pointy brow. "Tame Rosemary? She's a handful all right but I wouldn't have her any other way."

Robert chuckled inside. Good answer.

"Talking work fellas? You could always sing for

your supper." Rosemary sashayed down the stairs like a provocative Mae West in an old 1930s movie. She had a pen stuck in her mouth to mimic a cigarette holder and cradled a book in her arms. "I have my yearbook here and I want everyone to sign it."

Jane followed behind Rosemary. "Good idea. We should have an eighteen years later yearbook signing."

"I didn't know I was supposed to bring my yearbook," Darin said.

"Typical, Darin. It was on the invitation Jane sent out. You miss a lot by putting all your attention on numbers and dollar signs which leads to making rash decisions without examining the consequences." Rosemary plodded past him.

Darin smiled, then blinked as her statement registered. "Hey. I resent that." He stopped and looked at his friends. "Don't I?"

Everyone laughed and Arnold patted Darin on the back. "Do with it whatever you like, I'm going to get my yearbook."

Robert moved from the sitting area closer to the hallway and his room. The chenille spread and his L'Amour book beckoned. Jane waved at him. He pointed to himself to make certain she was motioning to him.

"My yearbook is in the trunk. Would you hand it to me?"

He nodded but hesitated at the hall entry, intrigued by Jane and her friends' interactions. Jane continued giving instructions.

"Put your books on the table in the sitting room so everyone can access them."

Darin piped up. "Jane, you missed your calling as an event planner."

"She's been writing lesson plans for years," Evan said.

Robert was beginning to get a bad taste in his mouth every time Evan opened his. Writing lesson plans for years should have meant she was better qualified for the kindergarten job than a newbie. But the way he said it made it sound like she'd been at it so long she should be put out to pasture, like a used-up racehorse.

Rosemary, who was growing on him in a good way, quipped, "Exactamundo. And you might want to give that some thought when you assign teaching jobs." Her brows arched above her huge winged out glass's rims—no simple accomplishment.

The way the conversation was going, Caroline's absence was probably a good thing.

"Administrative decisions are sometimes tough, but I have to be willing to make the calls."

Rosemary faced Evan. She held up her book and took the pen from her mouth. "Why not tell me all about it in my annual?"

Robert ducked into his room, leaving the door open, glad to retreat from the fray. He flipped the latches and opened Jane's trunk.

"Jane's things are in your room?"

Robert turned around.

Darin stood in the doorway. “Is she ... uh—”

“If you want to know if we bunk together. No.”

“Right. Boys downstairs and girls up, unless you’re married. I understand.”

“This trunk is heavy and has items needed for wedding activities. Jane left it here for convenience.”

“So ... you aren’t ... an item?”

Robert turned, gritting his teeth. He stooped to pull out the yearbook, noticed a diary underneath, then stood. “No. She is my coworker. That’s all.”

“Good. Well, I’ll be looking forward to becoming better acquainted with you.”

“Me too.” *Maybe.* Robert held out the yearbook. “Would you take this to her?”

Darin’s lips made a slight upturn. “Glad to.”

Robert glanced in the trunk at the dates in the diary—1995-2002. He gingerly flipped the pages of the diary. The book appeared to be more of a journal than daily entries. He placed the book back in the trunk and closed it.

Stepping back in the hall, he saw Caroline slowly descending the stairs. Had she waited for the topic of Evan’s job assignments to shift? The tension of Rosemary’s remarks had seemed to dissipate as general chitchat had resumed in the sitting room.

Rosemary held up her yearbook and said, “Listen to what Phillip wrote in my book our senior year. Roses are red, violets are blue; my life only has meaning when

I am with you." The sentiment received oohs and aahs. Rosemary lifted her glasses and made a show of wiping away tears. Then she grabbed Phillip by the collar and gave him a mind-numbing kiss. Boisterous cheers followed.

Jane clapped her hands. "While we have everyone gathered, now is a good time to go over the wedding activities planned for the weekend. Come find seats in the common room."

Cecelia took Arnold's hand. The couple seemed devoted to one another.

The large room could easily hold two hundred, depending on how it was arranged. Currently, it was organized on the perimeter with seating to read, play games or relax and enjoy the mountain view. Conversation groupings defined by natural woven carpets occupied the center. The seating area closest to the front entry was equipped with a TV in an entertainment center and a baby grand piano. A dining table for twelve was in the area next to the fireplace. Jane stood on the hearth.

"Gather around here." Jane motioned to the U-shaped seating formed by three couches and two wingback chairs.

Evan waved at Caroline to join him on the center couch. Phillip and Rosemary took the left and Cecelia and Arnold, the right. Robert folded himself into a wingback chair, ready to play his role as 'not an item'. Darin sat opposite him, eyes on Jane.

"You have this agenda in your welcome bags, so you don't have to take notes. I'll go over it. Let me know if you have questions."

"Yes, teacher." Rosemary elicited chuckles.

"First, food. Breakfast and lunch are on your own. Everyone signed up for items to bring and share so help yourselves. Dinner, I will prepare tonight, Cecelia and Arnold tomorrow, and then catered meals for rehearsal and wedding day will be delivered. I've posted house rules in the kitchen. Everyone please help as needed for cleanup."

"Me and Phil don't get to cook?"

"Nope. Everyone pitched in, so all you have to worry about is saying your 'I dos' and give us a chance to have some fun together."

"I'm game." Rosemary patted Phillip's knee. "How about you?"

With a nod, Phillip lifted his hands in resignation.

"This evening get ready for bride and groom bingo and some sing-a-longs. Tomorrow, put on your hiking shoes and we'll take to the trails. Later, you'll become songwriters. Then we'll enjoy a blast from the past with videos and gather around the fire pit for s'mores. Friday is crafting day, more on that later. Friday evening will be the bachelorette and bachelor parties. As best man you do have something planned, Darin?"

Darin stood and raised his fingers victory style. "Got it covered guys."

Jane shot him an apprehensive smile. "I thought you

might."

"Saturday is the sunrise wedding, followed by a celebration. Our task," Jane nodded toward Rosemary and Phillip, "will be to keep those two apart before the ceremony."

"Uncle Sam has been doing a good job of keeping us apart," Rosemary said with a pout.

"And we appreciate your service, Phil." Jane started clapping, and the others followed, standing to honor their friend.

Phillip waved and motioned for them to sit. "Guys, you know you're applauding a crazy bonehead that opted to endure miserable conditions."

The guy was far from a bonehead. Special Ops were highly trained in crucial operations. They had to be mentally and physically fit to make sound judgments and disciplined to never quit.

Rosemary shook her finger at him. "Take the compliments while you can, Baby. You know this bunch is stingy with them."

He smirked, a rare hint of cheer on his face.

Every time Robert looked in Phillip's direction, he furrowed his brow and his steely eyes locked onto Robert like radar. Phillip was the one guy Robert had interviewed from this group after the murder of Veronica Singletary. Martin Singletary let the investigators know Phillip had been involved in a theft and needed money to fulfill his dream to travel in Europe.

"Madam teacher, other instructions?" Darin asked.

"After the sunrise wedding and celebration Saturday, instead of waving off the newlyweds, Rosemary and Phillip will wave goodbye to us. So …"

Jane viewed her phone screen signaling a message, then a smile crept across her face. "I have a surprise. Hold on to your seats. I just received a text from Mr. Sing. He and his wife are at a nearby music camp maintaining Covid safety restrictions, and he's agreed to come for the wedding." She dropped the phone back in her pocket, a gleam in her eyes. "He'll be here tomorrow."

Darin stilled.

"That is a surprise …" Rosemary patted Phillip's hand. "… isn't it, sweet pea?"

He lifted his chin. "Yeah. I had no idea he was invited."

Scanning the expressions around the room, Jane's surprise could be better labeled as a shock. Robert wasn't sure if good or bad vibes were resonating in the shock waves.

Cecelia straightened and looked at her husband.

"Was it the music camp at Mountain Creek?" Arnold asked.

"I think he mentions the name." Jane pulled out her phone again and swiped the screen. "Yes. Mountain Creek."

"Our Amy attended the camp," Cecelia said, her brow furrowed. "Mr. Singletary was not listed as an instructor."

"He filled in for the scheduled instructor who had to cancel. Campers leave in the morning, and he will drive over."

"Imagine," Evan said, "your daughter is being trained by our teacher. We'll truly have the old ensemble together." He turned to Caroline. "Mr. Singletary, we called him Mr. Sing, was our chorus teacher and his wife was the drama teacher who taught us moves for show choir."

"I bet you're all thrilled." Caroline beamed.

"I invited him before the pandemic, and he didn't respond," Jane said. "But he called while I was upstairs and said he might work it out. I didn't want to get everyone's hopes up until I knew for sure."

"What about our quarantine?" Darin asked.

"Our daughter had to test and quarantine for camp just as we did." Arnold said.

Jane pointed to her phone. "Mr. Sing's text confirmed that all camp participants tested negative at the end of camp, making it safe to come."

Cecelia pushed back a side sweep of bangs from her eyes. "Where will they stay?"

"I tentatively set aside a first-floor double."

Phillip stood, rubbing his hands together, and managed a mirthless smile. "Looks like it's a done deal."

"Quite the news," Rosemary said. "You could have bowled me over with a blow-up beach ball. What's for dinner? I'll help." Rosemary nudged Jane and moved toward the kitchen. Cecelia and Arnold went to one of the private nooks and engaged in quiet conversation. Darin chatted with Caroline and Evan, who suggested they go out on the patio.

Phillip remained. He approached Robert and got right to the point. "Did you used to be a state agent?"

"Yes. I retired last year."

"You worked the Singletary murder and questioned me."

"I did."

He crossed his muscle-toned arms. The guy was a nightclub bouncer and Darth Vader rolled into one. "You better not be here to stir up trouble."

CHAPTER SIX

In the kitchen, Jane said, “Rosemary, level with me. What is going on? I’m getting less than positive vibes about Mr. Singletary’s coming.”

Rosemary wrapped her arm around Jane. “Let’s just say not all of us view him in the same way. When Mr. Sing took the job at a small private college on the other side of Montgomery ten years ago, many in Valleytown were happy. Some were happy for him, and some were happy he was leaving. As a chorus teacher, he was cream of the crop, but the personal side of him ...” Rosemary pushed her glasses to the bridge of her nose. “Do we need to wipe down food items and bring them in?”

“Caroline helped me clean and organize the only items we need right now.” Jane faced her friend. “Rosemary, come on. Talk to me. If I’ve pulled a big boner here, tell me. What about his personal side?"

Rosemary crossed her arms and plopped down on a counter stool. "Okay, here goes. Phillip was a juvenile offender on probation for stealing tires. Then Principal Jones caught him taking money from a drink machine at school. He liked Phillip and said he wouldn't report him if he finished his probation with no further incident. But when Veronica was murdered and money taken, Mr. Singletary brought up Phillip's theft and implicated him as a suspect. Mr. Jones "highly recommended," Rosemary used air quotes, "Phillip join the military, or he'd report the school violation. Mr. Singletary's insinuations derailed us."

"I didn't know."

Rosemary shrugged. "No sweat. You've been away from Valleytown a long time. When Phillip left, you missed me hooking up with the motorcycle mechanic. We had some kicks and almost got married but, he was no Phillip. Plus, the mechanic decided he liked the wife he divorced better."

Jane chuckled and sat down beside Rosemary. "I can see you sporting boots and a leather jacket."

"Phillip refers to the time in our history as my 'biker hiccup'. We both resented Mr. Singletary for a long time. But our relationship has strengthened through it all. Phillip has done well in the military. You could say we owe his success to Mr. Sing since his remarks were the catalyst sending Phillip on a more productive track."

"Then you're okay with him coming?"

"Sure. It's time to face our hard feelings and move on."

"That's a relief." Jane hugged her friend. The reaction to her announcement had not been at all what she had expected from her high school friends. But it gave her even more of an appreciation for Rosemary and Phillip and what they had overcome.

"We can't change the past, but we can use the past to mold our future."

The thought-provoking statement coming from fun-loving Rosemary brought the sting of tears to Jane's eyes.

Rosemary patted Jane's hand. "We'd better get dinner started."

Jane grabbed a napkin and dabbed her eyes. "Okay. I grouped spaghetti supplies beside the stove."

"Hello, ladies. Need an extra hand?" Darin walked into the kitchen. "I have untapped culinary skills."

"The only culinary skills I ever saw from you on choir trips was putting salt on your French fries," Rosemary said.

"I have progressed to the worldly condiments of soy sauce and Italian seasoning."

"Does that qualify him, Jane?"

"Sure. Ever made spaghetti sauce?"

"I know how to open a jar."

"What about chopping onion?"

"I can chop and cry with the best of them."

"Good. Here's the onions. Find a cutting board and go to it."

"Rosemary, could you wipe the items in the outside refrigerator and bring them in?"

Rosemary grabbed a box of sanitary wipes. "On it."

Jane pulled ground beef from the fridge and located a pot in a cabinet beside the stove while Darin went to the large porcelain sink and began peeling the outer skins from the onion under running water. "I've heard this helps prevent watering eyes."

Placing the cleaned items in the refrigerator, Rosemary said, "I'll tell you what works." She made circles with her fingers in front of her glasses. Kitchen goggles. I keep a pair of red and green goggles in my kitchen.

Darin shook his head. "Aren't your big old glasses shield enough?"

"You'd think. But the goggles have a foam fume seal. The water should help, though."

Jane started browning the ground beef. "Darin, I didn't exactly get shouts of praise when I announced Mr. Singletary would be here. What are your thoughts?"

"It will be nice to have us all together again."

"This is Jane, remember? I saw the look on your face. There's something bothering you."

"It's just ... well ... I belong to a private club in Montgomery. Correction. Past tense. Belonged to a private, invitation-only club. Mr. Singletary became a member through his first wife's well-connected family. Since his wife was murdered and they were not divorced, he was allowed to remain a member. But when Cynthia and I divorced, I was voted out. Mr. Singletary could have stood up for me but didn't. Losing my membership has been humbling and also cost me a couple of key business connections." He yanked at the onion skins with a vengeance. "You'd think being a part of the Valley Voices would have made a difference. But Mr. Singletary speaks up only when it benefits him."

"What do you mean?"

"Like casting suspicion away from him after his wife was murdered by making certain police knew students were aware of the four hundred in cash in his house."

Rosemary huffed. "Be glad you didn't have a juvey file or you might have been loaded on the bus to boot camp, like Phil."

"Why do you say suspicion was on Mr. Sing?" Jane asked.

"You're an investigator. The spouse is always the number one suspect." Darin began singing "Cry Me a River" as he chopped the onion using a rocking motion with a French knife.

The beef began to sizzle. Jane stewed over his remarks while breaking the meat into smaller chunks for browning. Darin's and Rosemary's attitude had taken her off guard. She'd have to ponder this later. Dinner had moved to the top of the agenda.

"You're a good chopper. Dump the onion in the pot."

"Told you I had untapped culinary skills."

"I won't let them go to waste." Jane pushed garlic, parsley, and mushrooms toward him. "Your reward is more to chop."

"Refrigerator items are cleaned and put away. What else do you need?"

"Open the cans of tomatoes and tomato sauce."

Cecelia came in with a subdued smile. "Do you need help in here?"

"Take over browning the meat and onion while I look for a large pot for the spaghetti."

"Check the rack hanging over the island," Darin said.

Jane stretched to pull down a large pot hanging by the handle but couldn't grasp it. Darin reached around her and unhooked it. His woody scent tweaked a memory of their dating days when he put his arms around her.

Robert cleared his throat behind her, and she jumped.

"Call for you. You left this on the hearth."

Jane took her phone. She shouldn't feel guilty but did. "This is Jane Carson."

"Hi. This is Amy Danford."

Why would Cecelia and Arnold's daughter be calling her? Jane put her hand over the speaker and said to Cecelia, "It's your daughter."

Cecelia frowned as Jane spoke. “Amy, hello. It’s been a long time.”

“I’m here at music camp with Mr. Singletary. He gave me your number and said I should talk to you first.”

“Talk about what?”

“Me coming him and his wife to the lodge. We have practiced a song as a surprise for Aunt Rosemary. She’s not my aunt, but it’s what I’ve always called her.”

Cecelia quit her meat browning task and gave Jane a questioning look. “I know you’ve followed quarantine protocol and I’d love to see you, but you better talk to your mother.” She handed the phone to Cecelia.

“Amy? … what in the world … slow down.”

Cecelia stepped out of the kitchen into the dining area. Rosemary filled the pot with water and placed it on the stove. Darin took over the meat browning job.

“I’d offer to help,” Robert said, “except I’ve always heard too many cooks can spoil the broth.”

Darin handed the wooden spoon back to Jane. “We’ve got dinner under control.”

“I see that.”

Robert’s tone as a non-boyfriend, pretending to be a boyfriend, was played to perfection.

“Robert, could you please check the firewood and make sure we have enough for the fire pit to make s’mores tomorrow night?” Jane asked.

“I’d be glad to.” Robert glanced back at Darin and turned to leave as Cecelia returned.

"Looks like Amy is coming too."

"Fantastic," Rosemary said. "If I could pick what I'd like my daughter to be like, it would be Amy."

"Amy and Rosemary have had a mutual admiration since Amy learned to make specialty coffees and smoothies at Rosemary's coffee shop." Cecelia smiled but Jane caught the twitch in the corner of her mouth as she handed the phone back to Jane. Being a parent with worries about children and following guidelines during a pandemic had to be a terrible burden.

Rosemary went to the kitchen door and called out. "Robert, ask Phil to help you with the firewood."

~

Outside, the breeze stirred the ash in the fire pit and troubled the trees. That was enough friction without bothering Phillip, who was in a three-way conversation with Evan and Caroline. After his warning, Robert doubted Phillip would care to help him do anything. Robert could handle firewood solo.

The fire pit held the black, charred remains of a log. He surveyed the area and saw a woodshed nestled between two oak trees where the edge of the lawn bordered the woods. He sprung the latch and sent a thumb-sized roach skittering under the rack, holding only two logs. An ax hung on a clip inside the door with a note.

When firewood runs low, please replenish.
You may cut fallen trees for firewood.

Return the ax when finished.

Robert unhooked the ax and took up the challenge.

Twigs and underbrush snapped underfoot, making his way through thickets and rocky ridges. The smell of composted leaf matter, fresh earth, and clean mountain air filled his nostrils. He was a woodsman on a mission. Nature was unspoiled and quiet here. No raking, mowing, or edging required. He descended a slope, stretching into a thick canopy of trees. To his right, he was rewarded with a fallen pine. Its branches scattered and trunk dry and brittle.

The rustling of undergrowth split the silence. Phillip plodded up behind him.

"Rosemary said to help you gather wood for the fire pit. I saw the note inside the door of the woodshed. Looks like you found a good specimen."

To keep a straight face, Robert had to re-channel his amusement about this tough guy taking orders from a zany redhead. He opted to brag on his find, "Perfect for lighter wood."

"I took you for a city fellow. You know about lighter wood?"

"I grew up on a farm. My grandpa taught me to look for an aged fallen pine with a strong pine scent."

"A farm is a place of learning not taught in books." The man didn't smile, but Robert caught the spark in his eye. "I'll chop. You gather branches and knots for kindling."

"Deal." Robert held the ax out to him.

The guy had muscles developed in places Robert didn't know existed. The way he whacked logs from the fallen tree trunk bordered on bionic strength. In less than thirty minutes, Evan had joined them, and they made it back to the woodshed each with an armload of wood more than sufficient for an evening around the campfire.

Inside, Jane was setting napkins and silverware on the dining table. "Wash up fellas. Dinner is ready."

At the table, Robert savored the herbed spaghetti sauce and garlic bread. Jane passed around a bowl of freshly sliced peaches, the aroma reminding him of their road trip and analysis of the murder case. Conversation shifted from facemasks and the coronavirus to high school memories. Robert settled for a side chat with Caroline.

"Jane and I stopped in Chilton County for these peaches."

"Alabama produces wonderful peaches. Peach squares were always a hit at 'Bama hosted events."

"I've never heard of peach squares."

"They're like little bite-sized peach pies and scrumptious. Mama's, off the beaten path in Tuscaloosa, fixes the best ones."

Her sweet southern drawl undoubtedly charmed kindergartners. With Jane's interest in research and history, he could see Evan's rationale to move her to teach older students. But Jane was not excited about the job change just as her friends didn't seem ecstatic about the chorus teacher joining them.

Compared to the excitement generated by Rosemary over Cecelia and Arnold's daughter coming, the news of the Singletarys coming to the lodge fell flat.

"Amy is my barista protégé," Rosemary said. "You show her one time how to make a coffee drink and she remembers it. Customers ask for the coffees she's invented. The girl has a creative knack."

"I know. Since the Stay-at-Home order my office has been in the corner of the living room and Amy presents me with her new creations all the time." Arnold wrinkled his forehead. "And not all her experiments taste great.

"You IT sorts are known to be unimaginative," Darin teased, "sure she's yours Arnold?"

Rosemary stood and clanged her tea glass with her fork. "I have an announcement. Phil and I are joining forces."

"I thought that was why we were here," Darin said.

"Not marriage. Business." Rosemary sat back down and pressed her shoulder to Phillip's. "Phil is opening a fitness center in the empty building next door to my coffee shop."

Phillip leaned back in his chair and draped his arm around Rosemary's shoulder. "We have two years to lay the groundwork while I finish my last duty assignment."

Rosemary patted Phillip's hand. "We wanted you to

be first to know and help us brainstorm business names."

Darin was quick. "Brawn and Brew?"

"Good one." Evan high-fived Darin.

"Maybe stress the fitness," Jane said. "Coffee and Conditioning?"

"Y'all sing. Maybe something like Bass and Treble." Caroline suggested.

"No." Phillip's response was quick and sharp.

Caroline flinched and Jane blinked. All remained silent for an instant. Caroline's suggestion made sense to Robert. This group had music as the common denominator. Now the mention of music created discomfort. First with the announcement of their chorus teacher coming, and then with the suggestion for Rosemary and Phillip's business. Why?

"Cute idea," Rosemary repositioned her glasses, "but might confuse people about our services."

"How about Sip and Tuck?" Robert said.

Rosemary slapped the table. "I like it. I'll fatten 'em and Phil can trim 'em. The perfect business combo."

Phillip offered the slightest upturn of a grin. After his duty assignments in Afghanistan, he might have to learn how to use his smile muscles again. Rosemary and Phillip proved opposites attract. Where he was steadfast, reserved, and surly she was pliable, bold and cheerful.

Brainstorming ideas for Rosemary and Phillip's business venture continued in a lighter vein, especially when Caroline came up with Eat Yummy and Trim Tummy.

"Speaking of yummy. I have yummy bars for dessert," Jane said.

"No kidding? The cookies your mom used to send for bus trips?" Darin asked.

"The same."

"Everybody, watch Rosemary," Evan said. "She always took more than her share."

"I did not." She peered over her glasses. "At least not always."

Evan poked Darin. "But I'm guessing you'd rather keep your eyes on Jane?"

Darin wiggled his eyebrows.

Was Robert stuck in a high school throwback?

"Robert, please get the DVD labeled number one with the papers attached from the trunk so Arnold can set it up for viewing."

Jane appeared to ignore the exchange between Evan and Darin. He'd best do the same. Inside the trunk in his room, he located two DVDs. Number one was hand labeled with the date June 7, 2002. Attached were several copies of Class of 2002 song lyrics. The second DVD had a production label: *Joint High School Choir Concert May 23, 2002*—the night of the murder.

Robert delivered the June 7th DVD to Arnold.

After the chewy dessert filled with chocolate chips, coconut and other stuff deserving of the name "yummy," everyone gathered in front of the television.

"I've copied excerpts from the graduation ceremony, so you won't have to suffer through the entire service, but you have to stand and sing the alma mater and senior class song. In case you forgot the words, I made copies." Jane gave the papers to Darin to pass around.

"Man, we're back in school again," Phillip said, and took a paper.

Darin walked past Robert, who had pulled up a chair to one side of the conversation grouping.

Robert raised his hand. "I'd like one, please."

"Sorry. I didn't see you."

Being invisible put Robert in a good place to observe. The video played and different members of the group made comments but the exchange between Evan and Phillip caught his attention.

"Look at Singletary," Evan whispered. "People thought he was wonderful to attend graduation after his wife was murdered."

Phillip nodded. "He soaked up the sympathy after he threw us under the bus."

"Certainly nixed our plans for Europe."

Rosemary punched Phillip. "Would you boys be quiet?"

Singletary on video led the alma mater. Jane stood. The others followed and their voices swelled and blended.

Robert didn't attempt to sing but enjoyed hearing them.

"Aw look. Here she comes," Evan said, "a young

Cecelia."

"You look just the same, except for the crazy cap." Darin held his hands to his head and mimicked Cecelia adjusting the mortar board on video.

"I was scared it was going to fall off," Cecelia said.

"Payback for sneaking off and getting married without telling us," Rosemary said.

"Shh. Listen." Jane had an unruly class. "Here's the song Cecelia composed with Mr. Sing."

On screen, Cecelia said, "This song is dedicated to the Class of 2002." Her voice was shaky but when she started singing, the words came out strong and clear. The group went silent as eighteen-year younger Cecelia sang solo on screen. Robert watched everyone's reactions.

Jane and Cecelia had trembling chins.

Arnold held Cecelia's hand and wore a smile of pride.

Caroline glanced at solemn Evan.

Rosemary wrapped Phillip in a side hug and rested her head on his shoulder. Phillip stood soldier straight, jaw set.

Darin, standing across from Jane, caught her attention and winked. Jane wiped at a tear trailing her cheek and smiled at him.

Robert understood camaraderie but something about Darin was off-putting. He had his sights set on Jane, yet Robert's gut questioned his sincerity. Jealousy? No. He didn't trust him.

Cecelia, on screen, invited the seniors to join in. The sound of the combined voices in the room jolted him as they sang:

Goodbye and farewell,
friends at Valley High.
We'll ne'er forget you,
and leave you with a sigh.

Oh, Valley High our treasure
your halls are glorious,
As we move on to life's unknowns
Please remember us.

For Valley High your teachings
Will ring forever true,
We'll always band together,
The Class of Two-Thousand-Two.

When the song finished, there were no dry eyes, Robert's included. But emotion generated from the song was not all he felt. A tense thread strung this group together. The whispered conversation between Phillip and Evan prickled his scalp—the telltale sign when a significant clue had surfaced. Puzzle pieces, but where did they fit?

CHAPTER SEVEN

The soft mattress sagged under Robert's weight. It should probably be turned to redistribute the stuffing. He needed to do the same with his own insides. Redo his inner thoughts. Shift around. Revamp and smooth over his outside feelings. He was an alien. A decoy of sorts planted as a pseudo boyfriend.

His Uncle Jim used to float a decoy duck in his pond to attract other ducks during duck hunting season. Decoy Duck Robert had attracted Duck Darin, and Jane no longer had to worry about looking like a wallflower. Robert was the wallflower. The tag along misfit, left to stew over the nagging murder case. He could get up and turn the mattress, but the diary inside the green trunk beckoned.

The diary covered the time frame of the murder. Perhaps Jane tucked the book in the trunk for him to look at and just failed to mention it to him with all the wedding activity. What would it hurt to look at what she'd written, strictly from a research point of view? There could be information to help in the murder case.

Jane would welcome the scrutiny of her writings if they benefitted the investigation. Right? Since she was busy with her friends, this was the opportune time to read her diary entries on the dates surrounding the murder. If he found anything useful, he'd discuss it with Jane.

He popped the trunk latches. The metallic clack sounded loud enough to be heard in the great room. He waited. Only laughter and singing drifted down the hall.

Easing the lid open, he pulled out the book with My Diary printed in embossed gold letters on the front. Opening the cover, a star made of cardboard slid out. On the back was SSR June 2, 1995. Jane would have been twelve. A Shooting Star remembrance?

He thumbed through the entries. She didn't write every day, apparently only writing when she had something to say. Impressed with her dedication, he located the section around May 23, 2002.

May 15- Tried to get Cecelia to spill and give us a sneak preview of the Senior Song she and Mr. Sing had been composing. No luck!!

May 16- I should have never signed up for PE my senior year. It was crazy hot, and my clothes were sticking to me by third period. No way I'm taking off my clothes and showering. Darin swears the guys have secret peepholes. I doubled up on deodorant and pulled my hair into a ponytail.

May 17- Raining. Got to walk around the gym 50 times for class. No sweat!

May 19- Hallelujah I got an A+ on my research paper on the selection of Supreme Court Justices. I'd have to totally mess up on the final to not get an A in American Govt. Mr. Euclid asked me to stay after class. I thought I was in trouble. But he complimented me on my paper and said I should consider a career involving history. I left on cloud nine. I do love research. Mr. Sing has us brushing up on the Gershwin Medley. We have to perform with some other high schools.

May 20- Rosemary is excited about the new Bruce Willis Die Hard movie. We're going (just us) this Saturday. Phillip acted hurt, but Evan said it was fine with him. It's fine cause he won't have to pay for my ticket. Some boyfriend.

Robert laughed out loud. She had him pegged.

May 21- We got our caps and gowns today. Rosemary was upset about the requirement to wear heels and a white dress that won't even show under the gown. Cecelia said she didn't own a white dress and didn't know where the money would come from to buy one. Her old car needs a new transmission. My last year's Easter dress should do.

May 23- Rosemary and Phillip were so cute singing "Our Love Is Here to Stay." Evan complains the songs are dorky, but I like the words.

May 24- Murdered! Mr. Sing's wife was found murdered last night. It's horrible to think we could have been singing "'S Wonderful" when she was fighting off an attacker. They think a burglar did it. Rosemary said Phillip was interviewed about money that was taken. Mrs. Singletary sometimes baked cookies for us to take on choir trips. Everyone feels so bad for Mr. Sing.

May 27- Seniors got to walk to the stadium for our class photo. Evan bragged a rich uncle gave him three hundred dollars. He plans to pool money with Darin and Phil to backpack in Europe. The band director helped us spell out 2002 on the field. I can't wait to get the picture.

May 28- I took attendance to the office first period. Saw a cute guy in a suit with a badge coming out of the principal's office. Bummer. Ms. Williams said some seniors might not graduate if they don't pass the final exam.

May 29- We got to wear our caps and gowns to Baccalaureate service at Valleytown Community Church. People talked about the murder and how we should slow down and appreciate each other more.

Rosemary wore a dress and didn't complain once.

June 2- Knock me over. Our first Shooting Star fell like a brick last night. Cecelia and Arnold ran off and got married. She'd been kind of quiet of late. She must have had eloping it on her mind. Of course, them getting married so fast set the PG rumor mill spinning. Rosemary and I plan to give them a big party.

June 5- My last exam. I actually teared up when I turned in my paper. High school is over, and I am Bama bound! Roll Tide!

June 9 Mom let me sleep all day. Senior Lock In after graduation was a blast. They gave out jillions of prizes. I won movie tickets for a year. Evan won a new pair of Nikes. I told him he could wear them walking around Europe, but he said the trip was off. Phillip decided to go into the military. Life is changing for us already.

Her remaining entries recounted final grades of all A's and preparation for college in the fall. Tucked in the back was the senior photo where the students formed 2002. Pretty impressive.

He closed the journal and slipped it back into the trunk. Jane mentioned Evan had acquired three hundred dollars. Add the fact with the whispered comment by Phillip tonight of being thrown under the bus by Singletary. Robert stood and ran his fingers through his hair. His scalp prodded him with a prickly alert.

Singletary's mention of the students overhearing there was four hundred dollars at his house should have been given more attention.

Robert had seen Martin Singletary as a liar. He'd decided Singletary was guilty based on his introducing suspects, discrepancies in his statements, and Robert's preconceived notions of how Singletary should have reacted to the murder of his wife.

He had learned over the years not to jump to conclusions, but clearly in this case he'd jumped in feet first. By zeroing in on Martin Singletary, he had left leads and interviews he should have followed up on incomplete. He had broken the rules. And a murderer was still on the loose.

If Robert was going to look at this case with fresh eyes, he needed to clear his head like an Etch-a-Sketch.

Pulling the three-ring murder book from his suitcase, Robert made a backrest out of his pillows and settled onto the cushy bed. He searched for the 'statements' tab and reread the interview of Martin Singletary conducted by lead Investigator Burgess and witnessed by Robert on the night of the murder.

He ran his finger across the words as he read and stopped at a quote from Singletary.

"I should never have said I'd put cash in my desk drawer at the house in front of the students. It was probably too much of a temptation ...But... No ... I refuse to think Phil ... just because a kid messes up..."

Casting blame. He let the police know there was the

possibility he goofed up in mentioning the money in front of Phillip, and Phillip might have taken it since Phillip had committed theft before and needed money.

Robert revisited his gut reaction. Suggesting who committed a crime was a typical ploy of the guilty to move suspicion away from them.

He scanned to the mention of the gun found on the floor next to his wife.

"She was scared because of the neighborhood break-ins. I bought the gun for her protection and now ... oh, God, she's dead."

Singletary's contorted face had seared into Robert's memory. During questioning, he collapsed in a chair in the living room, hung his head, and sobbed. When he raised his head, there was no sign of moisture in his eyes. At the time, Robert had deemed the display of emotion as acting. But Robert had learned over the years some people have trouble producing tears, even when their heart is broken. He'd experienced it himself, as if shock and grief suck you dry.

Robert turned to his follow up interview on May 25, 2002, with Singletary where he questioned him on discrepancies:

Q: On April 26—two weeks before the first neighborhood break-in on May 10—you purchased the gun found at the murder scene. Why did you state that you purchased the gun for your wife's protection because of the neighborhood break-ins?

A: That's not the only time we discussed the need for a gun. She was afraid of break-ins.

Q: You said your class heard the discussion with your wife about the four hundred dollars, but according to the school secretary, your wife was there during your planning period.

A: So what? My ensemble students often eat lunch in the choir room and heard the discussion. It wasn't a class, per se. Aren't you splitting hairs?

Q. I'll need the student's names who were in the choir room when you mentioned the money, if you can recall.

A. I know exactly who was there. Phillip Randoph, Arnold Danford, Evan Armstrong, Darin Foster, Rosemary Greene, and Cecelia Whitcom.

Q. You stated the reason you withdrew the four hundred in cash was for the upcoming summer choir camp, but the camp is two months away.

A. Haven't you ever heard of planning ahead?

Robert could still see the sneer on his face. Martin Singletary was smug and arrogant. Investigator Burgess had instructed Robert to follow up with the students. He spoke to Phillip, who had a juvenile record. Phillip admitted hearing about the money but was at the concert on the night of the murder.

Robert had dropped the ball and had never interviewed the other students. On May 29, Burgess conducted a follow-up interview with Phillip regarding an anonymous caller on the tips line. Phillip was seen spending a one-hundred-dollar bill. Asked where it came from, Phillip said he found it beside the bridge at Kriller's Landing.

Robert snapped the investigation book closed. He had done a shoddy job on this case. Phillip wasn't the only one associated with cash after the murder. According to Jane's diary, Evan had obtained unexpected cash, the guys had plans for Europe, and Cecelia needed money for her graduation dress.

Though Martin Singletary appeared to put his ensemble group in a vulnerable position to deflect guilt, he had given unpursued clues. Since the students and teacher were all at the concert, Robert had considered the leads as run to completion. Investigator Burgess had been sent on another case and left Robert to handle the final report in which he concluded that the death of Veronica Singletary was due to an apparent interrupted burglary by an unknown assailant.

Had his belief in Martin Singletary's guilt caused him to miss the truth?

~

Jane adjusted her T-shirt, pulled her ponytail tight with a scrunchie, and trotted down the wooden stairs in her running shoes for a day on the trails. When she reached the landing, she smelled coffee coming from the kitchen. She'd hoped to be the first one up, but somebody beat her to it.

She approached Robert's door. He'd left the group

early last night. She wanted to include him in the day's activities. Tapping lightly on the door, she said, "Robert, you up?"

"Just a minute."

She pictured him in pajamas, then wondered if he wore pajamas. The door opened. He had on jeans, a pullover shirt, and hiking boots.

"You're dressed for hiking."

"Wasn't I supposed to be?"

"Yes. Uh ... I was ready to have to coax you. You left the group early last night."

"Just giving you time to reminisce with your friends. But I know you have a schedule." He held up his copy.

"And we are supposed to be here together. Well, not together-together."

He held up his hand. "Save it. You don't have to explain to me. I wonder if there's such a thing as a trophy non-boyfriend-boyfriend. I feel used."

Jane rolled her eyes at him. "Oh, please."

He gave her his best smug grin. "Do I smell coffee?"

"I believe so."

In the kitchen, Rosemary, dressed in slippers and a robe, had the oven door cracked open and the buttery scent of oven-toasted bread added to the wake-up smell of brewed coffee.

"You're up? I thought I'd beat everyone to the kitchen this morning," Jane said.

"I'm an early riser and like my coffee before I get dressed."

Robert peeked into the oven. "I haven't had toast made in the oven in a long time."

Rosemary went to the refrigerator and pulled out a package of sliced cheese. "Slap cheese on these babies, put them back in the oven long enough to melt, and you've got my favorite breakfast."

"Sounds good. I'll help." Jane washed her hands at the sink.

"Where did you find the giant percolator?" Robert asked. "We searched the cupboards and only found that little stovetop model and had to consult the internet on how it worked."

"The urn was on the top shelf in the pantry. I figured in a lodge this size there had to be a bigger pot. Coffee's ready."

"Good deduction," Robert said.

"Thanks." Rosemary smiled. "Coming from an investigator that means something."

Jane smacked her forehead with the heel of her hand. "And we're supposed to be the detectives."

Robert's smirk told her he also felt the pang of stupidity. He went to the cupboard while Jane helped Rosemary peel cheese loose from the cellophane wrappers and place them on the bread.

"Ladies?" Robert raised empty ceramic mugs.

Jane nodded while Rosemary held up her own cup. "Thanks, but I've got mine already."

With cheese topping the toast, Rosemary slipped the baking sheet back in the oven. "It will only take a minute for the cheese to soften. You're dressed for hiking."

"Yes. I plan to make sandwiches for the hike, and everybody can pack anything else they want to bring," Jane said.

"We'll make an assembly line," Robert said, filling two coffee mugs.

"Let's eat first." Rosemary pulled the tray from the oven, placed the toast on a platter, and set it on the kitchen island.

"My rumbling stomach agrees," Jane said.

Robert slid a mug of steaming coffee in front of Jane, and she bit into the cheesy goodness of the toast.

Cecelia and Arnold came into the kitchen.

"I thought I smelled Rosemary's cheese toast." Cecelia pointed to her phone. "Amy texted. They'll be here in thirty minutes."

"Time for you two to join us. Coffee's on." Rosemary held up the platter. "Grab what you want. I can always make more."

"Phillip said to tell you he's on his way," Arnold said, taking toast from the platter.

"I'm excited Amy can come," Jane said. "She must have been around six or seven when I last saw her. Where does the time go?"

"It's hard to believe we've been out of school for eighteen years. But we're Shooting Stars forever." Rosemary stood and held out her hand. Jane joined her, along with Cecelia. Jane drew an invisible star with her index finger across the palm of Rosemary's hand. They repeated the gesture on each other, then high-fived as Phillip entered the kitchen.

Robert turned to Arnold, who shrugged and bit into his toast. "It's their secret handshake."

"The Shooting Stars rise again," Phillip said in his booming bass voice.

"The shooting stars rise again—sounds like song lyrics." Jane said. "Song writing is tonight's activity. Girls against the boys."

"Morning all." Evan walked in with Caroline and Darin close behind. "What are you talking about? Girls against the boys, for what?"

"Writing the best song," Jane said.

"We'll be a shoo-in with Mr. Singletary," Evan said.

"At least one good thing about his coming," Phillip mumbled.

"Don't forget. Cecelia wrote our senior song." Rosemary tossed a piece of cheese toast at Phillip. He caught it and hiked up a brow.

"Yeah, but with Mr. Singletary's help," Darin said.

Cecelia's face went solemn. Reminiscing over the senior song must still tug on her. "I was thinking Mr. and Mrs. Singletary would act as our judges," Jane said. "You boys don't want an unfair advantage, do you?"

"Absolutely," Darin said, and he and Evan fist bumped.

Jane shook her head and laughed at their antics. "We'll let him decide. Right now, we need to finish breakfast." Jane pointed to the binoculars hanging around Caroline's neck. "I see you're ready to take in the mountain view."

"Evan and I just saw a bright yellow goldfinch."

"At Eaglemont, shouldn't we be seeing eagles?" Darin asked.

"You are more likely to spot eagles in the winter months, December to early February. Goldfinches and their fledglings are active in the summer."

Caroline was a fountain of bird knowledge.

Evan's smile exuded pride over his new teacher hire. "Caroline tells me the goldfinch's call sounds like 'potato chip.'"

"Well, there's a bit of trivia I can use the next time I'm at a loss for words," Rosemary said.

"Is that going to happen anytime soon?" Phillip asked, crossing his arms.

Rosemary peered at Phillip over her feline inspired glasses frames. "Don't get your hopes up, sweet pea. Everyone, coffee is in the urn and more cheese toast is on the way." Rosemary got up and pulled out more bread to butter.

"Don't make more on my account." Caroline went to the fridge and took out a package of mixed fruit and some almond milk. "I always drink a protein smoothie for breakfast."

"Me too. She has me hooked on them now," Evan said.

"There may be a blender in one of the cabinets,"

Jane said. “I’ll look.”

“Thank you, but I always take my little bullet mixer with me when I travel.”

Of course, she did. Jane resisted rolling her eyes. She hadn’t noticed, but a bullet mixer and small can of protein powder sat in a corner beside the refrigerator. And who was this Evan who had always eaten triple cheeseburgers, the large size fries, and laughed at Jane’s suggesting he should eat healthier?

“I’m sorry I can’t go hiking. The only shoes I brought were flats,” Caroline announced.

Rosemary poked Evan. “You should have told her what to bring. It was in the instructions Jane sent. But then, of course, coming to a mountain lodge would tell most they’d need more than flats.” Then Rosemary whispered for Jane to hear, “Especially if her motto is ‘be prepared.’”

Jane pressed her lips together, hard. Rosemary made no secret of her irritation at Evan for giving this girl with the flawless complexion, blond precision cut hair, and a natural beauty mark underneath her left eye Jane’s position at school.

“You’ll miss out on some good exercise,” Rosemary said.

“No problem. I’ll do my yoga routine for exercise.”

“And you brought your exercise DVD?” Rosemary tapped her lips and asked the question which had formed in Jane’s mind as well.

“I did.”

With her perky reply, Jane could swear she saw a spark flash in Caroline's smile like those television toothpaste ads. Jane had to cover her mouth and choke down a giggle when Rosemary cocked a wide-eyed look at Jane.

Arnold, normally a man of few words, piped up. "Won't our creativity for songwriting be curtailed if we spend the day climbing a mountain?"

Phillip quipped, "He's got a point."

"Evan's staying here and doing my yoga routine with me. You could hang out here with us," Caroline said, measuring protein powder into her bullet mixer. "We plan to spend a pleasant time on the terrace bird watching."

Cecelia elbowed Arnold. "We're following Jane's plan and going hiking."

"And what Jane planned we will do." Rosemary gave a sharp look toward Phillip.

"Yes ma'am. I'm used to taking orders."

"I'm looking forward to hiking and hearing about Amy's music camp, aren't you?" Cecelia asked Arnold.

"It would be easier to talk to Amy on the terrace."

Jane's coffee had grown bitter. She slumped in her chair. Did anyone really want to go on the hike? Everyone should be excited to go hiking and take in the scenery, especially after being stuck inside so long with the pandemic. A hike should be a treat. Wrong.

"If no one wants to go—"

"Arnold is teasing you and me," Cecelia said.

"I am. And teasing Cece is my favorite pastime. It turns her cheeks pink." Arnold leaned over and gave Cecelia a kiss on the tip of her nose. She blushed. Blushed! After eighteen years of marriage.

"Whatever Jane scheduled, I want to do," Darin said, and winked at her.

"I'm in as well," Robert was gallant to add.

"Good." Jane pointed to Evan. "Since you are staying behind, will you prepare the fire pit for making s'mores tonight and gather sticks for roasting the marshmallows?"

"I had to learn how to gather and whittle sticks to teach my Brownie troop," Caroline said. "I'm somewhat of an expert now."

"You want to talk 'expert'—" Rosemary began but Phillip moved in and placed his hand on her elbow.

The doorbell chimed.

"Saved by the bell," Phillip said.

"Our favorite TV show in middle school," Cecelia added.

Caroline frowned. "Never heard of it."

Rosemary tilted her head back. "You were watching Sesame Street."

"Let's answer the door. It must be Mr. Singletary." Phillip steered Rosemary out of the kitchen as Caroline's bullet whirred into action.

"Shall we give Mr. Singletary our special ensemble greeting?" Darin grabbed Jane's hand. "Come on Valley Voices."

Jane turned to Robert.

"I'll take over the cheese toast operation." Robert gave her a thumbs up and waved her on.

With Darin at her side, Jane stood at the front door. She turned to the others gathered in a semi-circle behind them, straightening their clothes, and then standing erect.

"On three, when Jane opens the door, you know what to say," Darin said.

Jane wasn't sure who started the ritual but standing at attention and greeting their teacher at the beginning of class became a tradition their senior year. "One, two, three." Darin motioned to Jane to open the door.

"Good morning, Mr. Singletary," the group said in unison.

Mr. Singletary's blue eyes lit up, and a grin spread across his face. Except for a bit of gray at his temples and in his bristle beard, he was handsome as ever. Mrs. Singletary appeared much the same with a pleasant smile and good posture she preached when coaching show moves, but her hair instead of chestnut was now a stylish silver-gray shaped into a chin length curly style.

"Do we need masks, or can we hug?" Mr. Singletary asked.

"We've all followed the same protocol, so let's hope we're safe to hug." Jane hugged both Mr. and Mrs. Singletary.

Cecelia and Arnold grabbed Amy, who had hung back, in a bear hug. The pandemic had added a new layer of concern. Cecelia wiped at her tears. "Everyone, for those who haven't met her, this is our daughter, Amy."

"Wow, you could be sisters," Darin said.

"Good thing she takes after her mama," Evan said, patting Arnold on the back.

"Come on. You have two more to meet in the kitchen." Jane herded the three toward the kitchen where Caroline was pouring a purple concoction from her bullet and Robert was putting the bread in the oven.

"Mr. and Mrs. Singletary and Amy, meet Caroline Warner. She is a teacher and Evan's guest. And Robert Grey who is my guest and employer."

"Please, let me say up front, no Mr. and Mrs. nonsense. I am Martin and this is Rhoda. We even used first names at camp. Didn't we, Amy?"

Amy smiled and nodded.

"So, Martin, how many children do you and Rhoda have now?" Evan asked.

"We just have the one girl," Rhoda said.

"With the well-developed set of lungs she was born with, we decided one was very practical," Martin added.

"Nothing wrong with just one," Evan said. "I come from a long line of only children—my dad, mom, and me."

Martin turned to Robert and started to extend his hand, then offered his elbow. "I guess the elbow bump is more correct these days. Don't I know you?"

"We met years ago. I worked on your wife's murder case when I was a state agent."

His brows pulled close, creasing his forehead. "Yes. A terrible time. I do recall talking to you, but I've tried to block out those memories."

"Huh," Evan said. "I didn't realize you worked that case."

The aroma of the bread in the oven got stronger and Jane's knees weaker. "Robert, the toast?" So much for the murder case not coming up.

"Ah yes. Excuse me. I'm neglecting my duty."

"Mr. Singletary—" Jane began, but he interrupted.

"Martin. Everyone please, first names only. We want to enjoy the wedding as one of you."

"Martin, Rhoda ... this is going to be hard. Let me show you to your room. You will be downstairs and Amy, you will have a room to yourself next to your mom and dad upstairs."

"This place is fabulous." Amy flipped her hair to one side, just as Cecelia used to do. Walking next to her, with her teachers following behind, made Jane feel seventeen again.

Cecelia caught up to them. "I'll show Amy her room."

"Where are the bags?" Arnold asked Martin. "I'll help you. Jane has an activity planned for us at 10:00."

"Our bags are by the front door. What happens at 10:00?" Martin asked.

"We're going on a hike," Jane said. "I hope you'll

come."

"We're five years older but still raring to go, right, sweetheart?"

Rhoda smiled and nodded, but when he left with Arnold to gather their bags, the smile slid from her face. "Raring is not the word I'd use after winding up a weeklong camp and a two-hour drive."

"You certainly don't have to go on the hike," Jane said. "Evan is staying back with Caroline. She didn't bring any walking shoes."

"Martin really wants to participate with all of you." She sighed. "He's talked of little else since he got the invitation. Don't mind me. I'll freshen up and be ready to go, just maybe not raring."

"Good. Your room is right this way." Jane steered her toward the hallway.

"Tell me. This investigator you're with. Are you," she held up two fingers close together, "a couple?"

"No, no. He's my employer and came as my ... guest ... and friend ... not boyfriend." They came to room #102. "He'll be right across the hall from you."

Rhoda grimaced. "Sorry. I didn't mean to put you on the spot."

"No problem. I think you'll find the room comfortable. Let me know if you need anything."

Rhoda opened the door. "I'm sure it will be fine. I guess we'll see you shortly."

Jane walked back to the sitting room and plopped down on a cushioned chair. Rhoda's question did put her on the spot. Things within the group were awkward with Darin here solo and making overtures of pairing off with her. And though she didn't want anyone to think she was dating Robert; he was her guest and deserved to be treated as such.

Eaglemont was a grand place, but its grandness didn't prevent things from getting complicated.

CHAPTER EIGHT

The steps of a man are established by the Lord,
when he delights in his way;
Though he fall, he shall not be cast headlong,
for the Lord upholds his hand. (Ps. 37:23-24)

"Encouraging thought on a mountain top," Robert murmured, studying the inscription carved in stone beside the Eaglemont Boulder Trailhead.

"Listen up everyone." Jane's voice rose above the others.

He'd contemplate the deeper meaning later. Now was the time to see what Jane had in store for them.

Darin stood next to Jane. The rest of the group, minus Evan and Caroline, circled in.

"The hike to the mountain overlook is a little over two miles and considered an easy trail with only a moderate climb. I have a backpack with bandages, ointment, sunscreen and insect repellent in case you need them."

"Good thing. Us desk jockeys aren't fit like old Phillip," Darin said.

"That's why I assigned him to carry the lunch backpack." Jane held up a file folder. "I have handouts on the flora and fauna found in the area and the history of the overlook."

"I never knew a walk in the woods required all this preparation," Arnold said.

Robert smiled inside. He should see Jane's huge prepared-for-anything purse.

"Teach, I thought this was a vacation retreat." Phillip's comment prompted a quick jab to the ribs from Rosemary.

"I'd expect no less," Rhoda said. "Jane researched the costumes for the 1920s Gershwin performance, and you all looked authentic."

"Nostalgia time tonight. I brought the video of our Gershwin medley performance," Jane said.

"Good, we'll compare the past with the present," Martin added. He grabbed Amy's hand and held up her arm with his. "We'll be sharing a hand-picked song we practiced at music camp for the bride and groom."

Amy smiled shyly and gazed wide-eyed into Martin's eyes.

Rhoda's eyes narrowed.

"I'll take a handout," Darin said. "You can point things out to me along the way."

Robert questioned Darin's sidling up to Jane and flirting, like he was interested in her research. Especially since he was the old boyfriend who talked her into switching college majors before he broke up with her.

But Darin's attention to Jane shouldn't concern him. Robert was here as a warm body, so Jane wouldn't feel pitiful and single. He didn't understand the current mores of not attending a wedding alone. After all, Darin came alone. It must be different for a girl.

"Whoop. Whoop." Rosemary hooted and waved her handout. "Quicker we hit the trail, the quicker we get to see all the good stuff Janie wants to show us."

The group set out with Jane and Darin in the lead, followed by Phillip and Rosemary. Robert, now the loner, fell in behind them. He took in the musky scent of damp pine straw covering the path and slowed to answer a question from Arnold.

"So how long have you been in private investigations?"

"Two years."

"Investigations sounds exciting. I'm a fan of NCIS."

"Much of what they depict on television isn't how things really work, but it's entertaining."

Ahead, Rosemary stopped to pluck a yellow wildflower and stuck it behind her ear.

"Hey Rosemary, you've got a bee tracking you,"

Arnold said.

Robert avoided a bee, then glanced at a text alert from Vance.

Have the cold case DNA results. Call me.

Jane turned around and pointed. “Darin just spotted some bee activity around that hollow tree.”

Phillip pulled the blossom from Rosemary’s hair and tossed it. “No need to ask for trouble.”

Behind them Rhoda said, “Martin I’d better go back.”

“You sure? The bees won’t mess with you if you don’t mess with them.”

“I don’t want to take a chance of wrecking everyone’s good time if I get stung.”

“You have your EpiPen, don’t you?”

“I do. But a sting could still send me to the hospital. No need to run the chance.” She waved her hands. “Y’all go ahead.”

“We probably should move on past the hive,” Darin said, and nudged Jane forward.

“I need to return to the lodge to check on a text I just received,” Robert said. “I’ll walk with you and make sure you get back safely.”

“Appreciate it,” Martin said.

The others started walking. Jane and Darin were already out of sight.

“Tell Jane I’m going back, will you?” Robert asked Martin.

“I will.” Martin rushed up the trail and caught up

with Amy, who had lagged behind.

Rhoda watched Martin for an instant, her lips pursed in a thin line, then she turned and strode back toward the lodge.

Robert hurried to catch up. He'd make a stab at small talk. "Too bad about your allergy."

"I'd like to enjoy the butterflies and smell the sweet flowers on a walk in the forest, but I've learned to accept the hand I've been dealt."

Robert sensed the hand she'd been dealt included more than insect stings. "Did you have a good music camp?"

"Attendance was smaller than usual due to the coronavirus. We had a good time working one on one instead of with groups and we mixed in some online classes."

"Seeing young people develop their skills must be rewarding."

"Martin has a knack for recognizing and developing young talent."

Reaching the trailhead, Robert said. "We made it back, bee free."

"Thank you for returning with me."

"My pleasure. I've heard positive things about your husband and the ensemble from Jane. It must be a thrill for you to rejoin your old students along with Amy, one of the next generation."

Rhoda affirmed his comment with an "uh-huh" supported by little enthusiasm.

When they emerged from the trail, Evan and Caroline held up pointy sticks and waved.

Robert and Rhoda joined them on the patio.

"Back so soon?" Evan asked.

"We happened upon a beehive. Bees and I don't get along well," Rhoda said.

"Stings can be dangerous." Caroline rubbed and turned the point of a whittled stick against a rock. "A bunch of yellow jackets attacked my daddy, and he had a painful reaction. His face swelled and he had trouble breathing."

"Same here. I wound up in the hospital last encounter, and I didn't want to risk it happening today. Looks like you are doing well with your whittling project."

"We found a small grove of bamboo behind the greenhouse which is perfect for skewers."

"This bucket was behind the greenhouse too." Evan indicated with a nod toward the container filled with water. "Caroline reminded me to soak the skewers, so they don't burn."

Caroline's latest competence was useful, if for no other reason than to impress Evan. "Never know when those skills will come in handy," Robert said.

Caroline finished smoothing the end of a stick and handed it to Evan to place in the bucket. "Join us?"

"I believe I will," Rhoda said. "You can teach me how to whittle."

"Thanks for the invite but I need to make a call."

Curiosity about the DNA findings tempted Robert more than learning how to whittle.

Returning to his room, Robert grabbed the legal pad with case notes he'd been making and placed the call to Vance.

"You answered on the first ring. You must be in your office."

"I am. And in the midst of writing a report, which always makes me think of you, since you trained me."

"And you learned well. You called about DNA findings?"

"My boss man's boss man wants the cold cases given a new boost. As a result, he gave the green light to apply new discoveries in DNA testing to the evidence gathered in the Singletary case. The potential exists for solving a backlog of unresolved cases using new DNA analysis techniques along with the latest convicted offender samples. Chief Isler wants to use this case as a prototype."

"I did a poor job of investigation on this homicide, but if updated analysis provides information to find the murderer, it may become a model of cold case success and redemption. What have you got?"

"Hold up. Let me pull up the memo."

While waiting, Robert flipped to the page of notes where he'd requested analysis of samples from not only the murder scene but the neighborhood break-ins.

"Okay. Here are the findings," Vance said. "Burglary number one, 504 Wren Drive, Valleytown.

Discovered May 11, 2002. An unidentified fingerprint found on broken window glass at the scene, was run through the current Next Generation Identification (NGI)-FBI fingerprint system and is a match to Martin Singletary."

"His prints would show up in the system now because of the requirement for school employees to be printed?" Robert asked.

"Correct. Of course, his prints were obtained in his wife's murder case for elimination purposes also. Burglary number two, 613 Wren Drive, Valleytown, May 20, 2002. blood evidence on a piece of broken glass shows belongs to an unidentified female. Burglary number three is your cold case at 705 Wren Drive on May 23, 2002. Get this. A hair sample taken from the kitchen table matched the DNA of the unidentified female in the burglary number two."

"That finding validates Veronica Singletary's murder was connected to the break-ins in the neighborhood," Robert said. The report seemed to confirm the burglary-gone-bad scenario Martin had purported all along. Had he been wrong to distrust Martin?

"Analysis of hair samples on the victim's body, skin scrapings under the victim's fingernails and a broken fingernail beneath the victim belong to a different unidentified female. Neither of the female's DNA samples were in CODIS. So, if the females are repeat offenders they have stayed under the radar. The full report will be available to you in the chief's office when you return, but I'm giving you the crux of their findings."

Robert jittered the eraser end of his pencil against his yellow legal pad. "Thanks, Vance, as always."

"Sure. Oh, I almost forgot. Tell Jane I saw a guy from the Archives Department when I was at the capitol building yesterday. He said Jane should apply for the curator job and offered to hook her up with someone for a department tour if she wants. I'll email the link for the application."

"Thanks. I'll tell her."

"Text me if there is anything else I can do. You solve this one, and you'd be first choice to head up a cold case team—a whole new career for you."

"Your replay button is stuck, buddy. I am a long way from that happening."

Robert pulled the Singletary case file out and flipped to the burglary reports in the appendix.

The first burglary was discovered and reported by Martin Singletary. He stated the owners were out of town and he noticed their gate was unlatched and standing ajar. He went into the backyard and saw the window near the back door was broken. Since he was at the crime scene, he could have touched something.

But what about the female DNA discoveries at burglary #2 and #3? Had there been a female theft ring or possibly a gang with guys and girls and the girls left behind more physical evidence? Money seemed to be the target. Cash was taken from all three homes.

Robert reread the crime scene measurements and comments about the method of entry. All the forced entries were done by breaking a window by the rear door, reaching in and unlocking the door. But the distance from the broken window and the door lock in the Singletary case was forty-one inches. Too far away for a person to reach the lock, and a reason Robert thought the burglary had been staged when he was at the crime scene.

Investigator Burgess commented on the distance and Martin was quick to show how a sturdy stick could be used to reach over and push the lock open. Was he simply offering helpful suggestions or involved in a cover-up?

Now female DNA was connected to two of the break-ins, but unidentified. Did this mean the case conclusion had been correct and Veronica Singletary was the victim of an interrupted burglary by an unknown assailant? Had he reached another brick wall?

Robert flopped on his bed, making the bed springs screech. He grasped his hands and folded them over his forehead. Maybe he'd been looking at this mountaintop experience all wrong.

He was here for Jane. His purpose may be less about revisiting the murder case and more about Jane rekindling her relationships with old friends. She had always planned to return to Valleytown. Evan moving her out of the kindergarten job to fifth grade might be the direction she was meant to take. Or maybe losing the kindergarten job was the push she needed to apply for the museum job with the state.

Reviewing the homicide was secondary. But … maybe at the foot of Lookout Mountain, Robert was to step back and take an honest look at how he had handled the Singletary case.

Jane had called him out for not following his own rules. She was right. He did not have the experience he'd gained over the years when he was assigned to the murder investigation. Personal opinion could color a case. Sticking to facts and staying open to all leads was critical to an investigation. He had seen occasions when a different investigator, or even the same investigator viewing evidence from a different perspective, could produce a break in a case.

Robert sat up and swung his feet to the floor. Face it. Bottom line. This was the business he was in, the business of solving cases.

Affliction or blessing, he was a detective and detectives didn't have an off switch. He could still see Veronica Singletary lying dead on her kitchen floor. A life ended too soon. And the murderer had gone free—for eighteen years. The cold leads had new sparks with the DNA report. He had not been thorough in his investigation. Females were involved and likely more than one person was at the scene of the crime. With new clues, the case had moved back into the forefront of his mind.

He couldn't deny the rush of excitement at the

thought of digging into clues and reevaluating what was done. More importantly, he wanted to apply his experience to tie up loose ends. There were questions he had never pursued. Incredibly, the players of interest were currently at his disposal. Sort of. Accessing them discreetly was a problem.

Robert stood and paced. Why was he here?

Lord, I need wisdom. The inscription on the rock beside the trail says the steps of a man are established by the Lord and it's delightful to follow His way. I'd be delighted to have you order my steps and claim that promise.

Robert sat at the desk, quieted himself, and closed his eyes.

Jumbled thoughts goaded him. Work the cold case and risk upsetting Jane? Tell Jane about the curator job? Remain invisible and play non-boyfriend? The tangle came to rest on one common thread—Jane. Robert had to come to grips with her leaving and the impact it would have on the agency.

Life would be less complicated. No more saving her from drug runners, scaling gates and buildings to extricate her from insurgents, or rescuing her from rat-infested mansions. His days could return to the mundane.

But what would he do without her to complicate his life? She'd become a real partner, and he'd miss her. However, wishing her to stay on was probably a bad idea. He'd have a hard time keeping his feelings on a professional plane and the proof was in his reaction to her old boyfriend.

Robert pushed the flower-patterned curtains back and could just see the edge of the trail where Jane and Darin had paired off and were hiking together. Was this what jealousy felt like? Miserable and out of sorts? The idea smacked him square in the chest. Jealousy did not wear well on him. Jane may not be staying with the agency, and he'd have to accept the fact. But he didn't want her to settle for the guy who'd dropped her and was trying to snake his way back into her life.

He and Jane were at a crossroads. Was this the reason they were brought to this mountain top? Were they both supposed to revisit their pasts?

He'd like to help Jane find her next steps—but Lord help him—he'd have trouble encouraging any steps for Jane that included Darin.

~

Jane laughed at Darin's retelling of finding Houndstooth, the cat, while they were at the University of Alabama.

"The flea covered critter yowled and hissed when we dunked her in the bathtub. I tried to turn her loose, but I couldn't. Her claws were embedded, and we all got a bath." Darin held out his arm and pointed out marks he claimed to be scars.

Jane inspected his arm. "Those are freckles."

Darin shrugged; his smile sheepish. "The freckles must have covered the scars."

"I wonder what happened to the cat."

"Seeing the old stomping grounds with you would be fun." Darin took Jane's hand. "When the pandemic is over, we should take a road trip and find out."

Darin holding her hand brought old feelings rushing in with red flags attached. So engrossed in forging ahead and telling old college stories, Jane realized she hadn't heard the others on the trail behind them for a while.

"The trail splits ahead. We must be going too fast."

"Or they're going too slow."

She'd left everyone, including Robert. "I should have paid closer attention. What if something's happened to Rhoda?"

"They'd let us know. I'll bet they're studying your flora and fauna sheets and will catch up."

"No. We'd better go back."

Jane retraced their steps to the last bend in the trail when she heard Rosemary's signature laughter.

"See? Rosemary's laughing. All is well."

"We'll wait here for them. We should have taken time to identify trees and plants along the way."

"I'm enjoying this bit of alone time with you." Darin swept off the flat surface of a boulder large enough for the two of them to sit on. He drew in a deep breath. "I love the smell of the forest."

"I read five hours a month in a forest will greatly improve your mental health. New growth springing from damp moss and decaying trees creates a calm repose, even on a hot summer day."

"It's not the vegetation, but you who improves my mental health," Darin said.

Jane snort laughed. "You've got to be kidding. You're hurting if your mental health depends on me."

"I'm not kidding. Reflecting back, we've shared some really good times. Like late night pizza."

"Studying in the library," Jane added.

"Cheering for our team."

"Coffee breaks during final exams."

"Now we're together again, it seems more like days than years have gone by."

"Um … in a way … yet when I reflect on work and the strain of struggles last year with my mother's sickness and death, it makes high school and college seem like ancient history."

Rosemary's laughter tinted the air that had grown too close around them.

"Rosemary and Phil's love bridged the gap." Darin's shoulder brushed against hers.

Jane shifted on the hard seat. "There's something I wanted to talk to you about."

"Same here, but you go first."

What was with his dimpled grin? The one that used to melt her toes into mush. Of course, the melting occurred before he dumped frigid water on her, said he'd met someone else, and froze her toes to brittle bits.

"You're Phillip's best man. I assume you've planned a bachelor party ... well, I hope it's not noisy and ... in good taste."

"You mean I need to cancel the naked lady popping out of a cake?"

She whacked his shoulder. "Don't tease. I just want things to run smoothly."

"Jane," Darin settled his hand on her knee, "that's what I love about you. You are gracious and always worry about others." He turned to face her. "I have to say this. I can see I made a mistake in letting you go. I'm asking for a second chance."

Her pulse pounded, numbing her thinking. Jane opened her mouth to speak but didn't know what to say. He tapped her lips to shush her.

"I don't deserve another chance. I do deserve to have you spit in my eye." He lifted his chin and leaned toward her, making it easy for her to serve up retribution, but made her laugh instead.

"Don't be a goof …" She turned away at the sound of approaching voices.

He touched her hand. "I've planned a very respectable evening for Phil. We'll talk more later?"

"Sure. Let's check on the others."

Rosemary with Phillip rounded the bend first. "There you are. We thought we'd lost you."

"Sorry. We were chatting and shouldn't have left you." Jane slid from her perch on the boulder. Darin stood and rested his hand at the small of her back. "The trail divides ahead, and we go to the right. Are you enjoying the walk?"

Cecelia and Arnold joined them, followed by Martin and Amy.

"We are." Arnold waggled his handout. "Confession. Sorry I needled you about the handout, Jane. We're enjoying matching plants and trees to your descriptions."

"The scenery is beautiful and cooler," Amy said.

The forest tempered the hot June weather. "Nature's air conditioning." Jane craned to look behind them. "Where's Robert?"

"He accompanied Rhoda back to the lodge after we saw the bees," Martin said.

"Bees shouldn't attack unless threatened."

"She knows, but steers clear just in case. A bad reaction landed her in the emergency room once. She insisted we keep going and Robert was kind enough to escort her back."

"He's not coming at all?"

"Said to tell you he had to return a phone call, and he'd see you back at the lodge."

Jane's heart sank. She'd really wanted to share the mountain view with him. He'd been so good about being on the periphery of things and playing the part of the not-a-boyfriend employer. She didn't want him left out. "I hate that they can't make it. We'd better stick close together until we reach the overlook."

For the next thirty minutes, the group negotiated rocky patches and climbed over the large trunk of a fallen tree. Then the peak of the trail opened to a broad meadow. A huge boulder jutted out over the mountainside, giving way to a panoramic view of rolling green mountains in the distance. Gasps of oohs and aahs came from the group at the sight. The scent of rhododendron blossoms hung in the air and clusters of brilliant pink flowers colored the hillside. Overhead, the sky was clear and bright blue.

"Look at this." Jane motioned everyone over to a flat surface on the side of the boulder. She ran her hand across the rough etching carved into the rock. "I read about this inscription on the website when I booked the lodge. It's exciting to actually see it."

The little group gathered behind Jane.

"What does it say?" Amy asked.

"They shall mount up with wings like eagles."

"Sounds like poetry," Amy smiled at Martin. He returned her smile.

"The words come from Scripture in the Bible," Phillip said. "Those who wait for the Lord shall renew their strength, they shall mount up with wings like eagles, they shall run and not be weary, they shall walk and not faint." His deep voice, quoting the words, sent a shiver of inspiration through Jane. A reverent silence fell over the group.

"The verses got me through more than one tight spot during attacks in Afghanistan."

Rosemary grabbed his hand and leaned her head against his shoulder. "And to think the verse is a part of our wedding weekend."

The extraordinary moment settled on them like the soft hug of a morning mist. Darin wrapped his arm around Jane's shoulder.

Jane had been praying for God's path in her life since the time for leaving the investigations agency approached. Had she been brought to this place with old friends to find her direction?

Honestly, she'd been dreading the return to the kindergarten classroom. Was teaching the older students the challenge she was meant to tackle? Or was it a signal her life was destined for something entirely different … and unexpected?

Unexpected would describe the day Darin had asked her to meet him at Denny Chimes on the quad of the UA campus.

"Jane, we've been through a lot of great times together," was the way he started his bombshell. "I consider you my best friend, so I wanted you to be the first to know. I've met the one."

"The one?"

"The one I want to marry."

Jane had beamed, thinking he meant her.

Then he spouted out her name. "Cynthia Hightower. She goes to Samford and is entering Cumberland Law School. I met her when I interviewed with her father who is president of the People's Trust Bank in Montgomery. Jane, you'd flip at the size of the conference room. I owe it all to you."

"Owe me?" She sputtered. "How?"

"You're my buddy. You kept me on the straight and narrow. Made me study and didn't let me get distracted by dating a bunch of girls. Then pointed out this job."

Buddy? She thought he was her boyfriend. Isn't that what you called the guy you dated for four years?

"You should see the Hightower's house—mansion, I should say. Mr. Hightower invited me to dinner and when Cynthia walked into the room, it was love at first sight. There is no other way to describe it."

Jane had another way to describe "it." Dumped on, humiliated, injured, stepped on, and cut to the quick. When he had asked to speak to her on the campus green, she'd thought he was going to tell her about a great job offer ... or propose.

What was worse, the guy was so into himself he was oblivious to her feelings. He really believed she'd be excited for him.

Had the years in the work world since college changed Darin and his values? With his apology, could there be a future for her and Darin now? Having the Valley Voices together again was bringing back memories long forgotten. She thought she was over Darin.

But they had picked up where they left off. Memories only they could appreciate were surfacing. A bond experienced in teen years was strong adhesive. Darin and Jane shared a unique connectedness.

Rosemary and Phillip were proving young love could be rekindled.

Was it possible to restore the lost years? Is that why she was here?

But what about Robert? Was there, or could there be, anything beyond friendship for them? He might be her boss, but she couldn't deny the strong bond between them. Was she here to sort out feelings, past and present? Or was she missing the fact that Robert could be here solely to revive his investigative career?

Lord, make the route for Robert and me clear as the blue sky above.

CHAPTER NINE

A dark cloud merged into a spiraling tornado. The twisting and turning became a swarm of giant bees jetting around him. The buzzing vibrated in his head and turned into cackles. Helpless, Robert lay beneath the onslaught. The buzzing turned to mockery, shouting his name. He felt pressure on his chest. It was hard to breathe. Had he been stung? The pressure moved to his arm.

"Robert. Robert."

The bees receded into blackness. The pressure lifted from his chest. Robert forced his eyes open. Jane's wrinkled forehead and inquiring eyes were inches from his face.

"Hey. You fell asleep with this murder book draped over your chest. I was worried when you didn't answer the door and came in."

Robert sat up. "The murder case mixed with Rhoda's bee concerns produced a weird dream."

"We just returned from the hike, and everyone is freshening up before starting the get-to-know-the-bride-and-groom activity. I saved you a sandwich in case you didn't eat. Shake off the weirdness and come join us."

Robert smoothed his hair, trying to clear his head. "Add a Dr. Pepper and I'll play your silly game."

Jane lit up. "Wow. I was ready to beg."

He sighed heavily. "Save your begging energy. You may need it later. My stomach is urging me to feed it." Plus, he'd decided to do some rapport building. Working on good interpersonal relationships might open doors for him to converse with her friends about the time surrounding the murder.

"Good. I'll take you however I can get you."

"I'm not so sure you need me as a token-guy anymore.

"Sure, I do."

"Darin is ready to step in."

Jane cocked her head, then turned and walked to the door. Her non-answer to his remark filled the distance she put between them. Did his remark not dignify an answer, or was it on target?

"I'll get your Dr. Pepper and meet you in the great room," she said and left.

He brushed his hair and attempted to plaster down his pesky cowlick with water. The tuft of hair on his crown laid down a moment then popped up like a jackin-the-box. He tossed his comb on the sink. “Forget it.” He tugged on his shoes and ventured out of the room.

After downing his sandwich and drink. He joined the group where Jane stood in front of the fireplace in teacher mode with pencils and paper in hand. The heady fragrance from rhododendrons someone must have picked on the hike, scented the room.

“Cecelia and Arnold host tonight’s dinner, followed by making your own dessert of s’mores around the campfire. In the meantime, I have an afternoon of wedding activities for you.”

“Why aren’t you in the kitchen slaving over a hot stove?” Evan asked Arnold.

“Because I have a smart wife.”

“We have an easy meal to prepare. We don’t want to miss the fun,” Cecelia said.

“The fun will be seeing how well you know the bride and groom,” Jane said. “Robert and Caroline, even though you just met Rosemary and Phillip, you play too.”

Robert rubbed his hands together. “Can’t wait.” He smirked and held out his hand.

Jane eyed him, shook her head, and gave him paper and pencil.

Handing Darin the additional paper and pencils, she said, “Would you hand these out for me?”

“Sure thing.” Darin pushed out of his chair and winked at Jane. Robert couldn’t see her response. Darin needed a smooth operator sign hung around his neck.

"I asked the questions of Rosemary and Phillip two weeks ago. Fill in the response you think each made. There is a food bank of choices to pick from at the top. But I warn you, I put in some extras to fool you."

Evan clicked his tongue. "Sneaky."

Robert viewed the questions which asked for their favorite car, color, ice cream flavor, fried food and movie.

"It's hard to think of liking a fried food," Caroline said.

"Are you sure you're a southerner?" Rosemary asked.

"Fried is so bad for you."

"I bet you order salad at McDonald's," Rosemary muttered while working on marking her paper.

"The garden salad is the best," Caroline said.

Rosemary bobbled her head and rattled her paper. "I knew it."

Jane giggled. "Rosemary, no need to mark your answers, only those about Phillip. We'll see how well you know each other after eighteen years."

"He's been buddied up with Uncle Sam most of those years but I'm thinkin' I know my man."

Robert worked on his answers for Rosemary first. He scrolled through the suggested words. She was outgoing, talkative, and enthusiastic. Of the choices for car, he selected Volkswagen bug. He could see her flitting around town in a VW. Favorite color had to be something bright. He checked red because of her red glasses frames. Fried food. French fries were tempting, but this was Rosemary. He picked onion rings. Ice cream. No way her favorite was plain vanilla. He chose Rocky Road. Movie, likely a superhero because of her admiration for Phillip. He selected *Spiderman,* since he wears a lot of red.

"Honor system. Check your own papers." Jane read the answers. "Phillip, how did you do?"

He shook his head. "Missed one. I thought you loved "*Lord of the Rings*.""

"I do. But Peter Parker is so adorable as Spiderman." Rosemary wiggled her eyebrows. "At least I'm able to keep my man guessing, so he won't get bored."

"Rosie, I am certain life with you will never be labeled boring."

"Anyone get all of Rosemary's answers correct?"

Robert raised his pencil.

Jane smiled. "Robert is a good people analyzer. Your prize, Mr. Grey, is Rocky Road popcorn, the flavor of Rosemary's favorite ice cream."

Jane handed him a bag of popcorn and read the first answer for Phillip's choices. "Favorite color: blue."

Rosemary hollered, "No way."

"What do you mean? I answered blue."

Their face off amused Robert, and Rosemary wasn't giving up.

"You answered wrong."

Phillip flopped his paper in his lap. "Okay. What's my favorite color?"

"Black. Look at you. You're wearing a black T-shirt, a black cap, and black shoes. We were almost late to our last high school concert 'cause you had to stop and clean your black shoes. I tried to get you to just change them …" She stopped.

Phillip's eyes bore into her for an instant. Then he said, "I'm wearing blue jeans."

She huffed and sank back onto the couch "Jeans don't count, blue is their normal color."

"So says Rosemary's logic," Evan said.

"Are you going to argue about my favorite car?"

"Maybe. Depends on what you answered."

"Suburban," Jane said.

Rosemary stomped her foot. "You know you drool all over yourself when you see a Mustang."

Phillip grinned and shrugged.

"Favorite ice cream: Chocolate."

"I got that one," Darin said.

"I did too." Rosemary gave Darin a fist bump.

Jane continued. "Fried food. French fries."

"Yes." Rosemary slapped Phillip's leg.

"Ouch." Phillip rubbed his thigh. "I hope you care for me enough to lighten up and not slug me if you don't get my favorite movie."

"Only if you don't put what I did."

"Movie: *Matrix*."

Phillip leaned away from Rosemary. She grasped and turned his head to face her and planted a serious kiss on his lips.

Martin laughed. “I think he gave the right answer.”

“When I first heard about *Matrix*,” Darin said, “I expected just another sci-fi action thriller with special effects.”

“Me too, but the movie has a plot as well,” Arnold said.

“Exactly. With characters that you care about.”

“Looks like we have two movie critics,” Jane said, and smiled at Darin. “Did anyone answer all of Phillip’s favorites correctly?”

Robert felt strange but was the only one to lift his pencil.

“You got them all again? Congratulations.”

“I guess that’s why you’re a detective,” Caroline said.

“You know my man better than me. Whenever I have trouble figuring out what he’s thinking, I’ll call.”

“He’s an amazing investigator,” Jane said. “Your reward is a DVD of Phillip’s favorite movie. And no one despair if you missed out on winning a prize, you have another chance.”

“Ask me Rosemary’s favorite guy and I’m a cinch to win,” Evan said.

“This is more of a challenge and will be guys versus girls. Everyone will have ninety minutes to write a song. Girls will draw one tune from the Gershwin musical the chorus performed and a favorite from Rosemary’s list. Guys you will do the same except you draw from Phillip’s favorites list. The task is to compose a song about the favorite item to the tune of the Gershwin song."

"We'll let the bride and groom draw the tune and topic. Rhoda and Martin have agreed to be impartial judges of the best song. Girls will compose using the keyboard Martin graciously loaned us. Guys you have the piano."

Compose a song? This was a first for Robert in rapport building. But who knew what doors might open? He'd observed fellowship develop in a piano bar, but booze and cigarette smoking were the usual accompaniment.

Robert got up and moved with the rest of the men gathering around the piano. "Fellas, I hate to tell you but my elective in high school was woodworking. The closest I came to making music was the sound of pounding nails. Zero music talent here."

"No sweat. We'll use your intuitive talents," Phillip said.

"Contestants, get ready to draw your tune and topic." Martin held up his watch. "Begin."

Darin held up the slips of paper. "Okay Phil. Choose our tune and topic."

Phillip read from the first slip. "'S Wonderful."

"One of my favorites," Evan said.

Robert grimaced. "Unknown to me."

"No problem. This song is imprinted on our hearts," Darin said. "What about the topic, Phillip?"

Phillip pulled another slip. "French fries."

"'S marvelous," Darin said, and chuckled at his joke.

Darin sat at the piano and fingered the melody. He was a financial guy who not only cooked and schmoozed but also played the piano.

"What rhymes with fries?"

"How about lies?" Robert said.

Phillip shot him a look as if he'd selected the word to annoy him.

Darin shrugged. "Lies—a possibility—better than flies."

Arnold tapped his watch. "Time's ticking. The girls are hard at it."

With Cecelia at the keyboard, laughter and music were coming from the girl's end of the room.

"Let's divide the responsibility," Darin said. "Arnold, you and Robert work on words that rhyme with French and fries. Evan and Phillip, we can work on the chorus.

"Bench, cinch, trench," Robert offered.

Arnold jotted down the ideas and handed them to the guys working on the chorus.

"Fries are potatoes," Arnold said. "How about potato/tomato?"

"Or spud and dud." Robert was gaining creative steam. "France is a country in Europe. Think of the European places you wanted to roam after graduation."

"The guys did talk about going to Europe—"

Darin interrupted Arnold. "We discussed backpacking in Europe. How would you know?"

"Talk I heard when I worked the Singletary case. Ever make it to Europe?"

"Uh ... no," Darin said. "Except Phillip. You had an all-expense paid trip to Germany, right?"

Phillip nodded, and his frown morphed into a scowl.

"Name some countries near France." Robert said.

"Greece." Arnold said.

"Did you ever go?" Robert asked Arnold.

"Me? No. Closest I came to Greece was in the bottom of a skillet."

Evan patted Arnold on the back. "He remained cozy in Valleytown. The first of us to be in a family way. Hard to believe Amy is the age we were during our chorus days."

Arnold took a swallow from a bottle of water. He turned his head to cough, then turned back. "It is hard to believe."

Did the mention of the early arrival of their baby make Arnold nervous? Robert tried a different tack. "Maybe think of landmarks in France. Eiffel tower?"

"Mona Lisa. Is she French?" Darin asked.

"If she weren't our competition, you could ask Jane," Robert said. "She is big on historical research."

"I forgot. She is big on historical stuff." Darin's eyes lit up.

"You have one hour left," Martin announced.

"We better go with the ideas we've got, guys," Evan said. "Time waits for no one."

An unstoppable truth.

~

"Time." Rhoda said.

The plink of musical keys and voices quieted. Jane's chest felt light, seeing the smiles on faces around the room. More than hoping the crazy song she and the other girls had composed would win acclaim, she was pleased Robert had engaged in the activity with the guys.

"Ladies first," Rhoda said. "Men, gather closer."

Rosemary plucked a rhododendron stalk from the vase on the table and mimicked using it as a microphone. "Our tune from George and Ira Gershwin is "Nice Work if You Can Get It," and the topic is the world's most ingenious culinary treat in the fried food group—that is a food group, right? The round, crisp, tasty delicacy—the onion ring. Feast your ears on this, boys."

Cecelia played the intro.

"No fair. You've got a piano teacher on your team," Evan said.

"Hey, all is fair in love and war." Rosemary waved the flower at Evan. "Besides, Darin plays the piano."

"Yeah, but—"

"Evan, sit," Phillip said. "Let them have their piano teacher. They probably needed extra help. Be nice and listen." He looked at Rosemary. "Give us what you've got."

"You sure you're ready?"

"Yes, dear."

"After that rude interruption, we shall present, 'The Onion Ring Song,' Hit it, Cecelia."

Jane squeezed in tight with Caroline and Amy around Rosemary's make-shift mic. She held up the one copy of the song to read from. Jane stumbled over a few of the words, but Rosemary's robust voice carried them through.

"Going with my baby
to a party the other night,
it should have been a good time,
but almost ended in a fight.
Sitting with my main man,
hoping to dance and sing.
He only wanted one thing,
and the one thing was onion rings.
He asked me to pass ketchup,
salt and pepper too.
It's all that I heard from him,
as the time he wasted grew.
The night was going nowhere.
I had to take a chance.
I decided to not sit there,
and invented a brand-new dance.
Finally, I got him
to join in and dance and sing.
Now we're doing our own thing,
it's called The Onion Ring."

Rosemary stepped up on the big square table in front of the fireplace and shouted, "One more time!"

Cecelia played the tune again, and Jane sang with fervor alongside the others.

When they reached, "Finally I got him," Rosemary whipped her pointer finger at Phillip. She stepped off the hearth. "To join in dance and sing." She pulled Phillip to his feet. With her arms making a circle above her head, Rosemary danced around him. "Now we're doing our own thing." She twirled in a circle. "It's called The Onion Ring."

Cecelia ended the song, running notes up the keyboard. Martin and Rhoda stood and clapped. Jane checked Robert's reaction. He and the rest of the male competition rewarded them with hoots and applause.

"Oh my," Martin said. "What a show. Get ready for the Recording Academy to come knocking, ladies."

"But before you do, move to the piano," Darin said.

Jane moved with the girls as a group to the opposite end of the room and she sat up front, close to the piano.

"Hey, judge," Evan called out to Martin, "what happened to being impartial?"

"Well … it's always nice to defer to the ladies," Martin said.

"Deference," Evan said in a whisper to Darin, "is that what it's called these days?"

Darin snickered. "I thought the word was dalliance."

Phillip shushed them.

What were they talking about?

"Now let's hear from the challengers," Martin said.

Evan stepped forward. "Enough of the pleasantries afforded the ladies. I admit they made a fine attempt at songwriting. But now you will hear the real deal."

Rosemary stood. "Give it a try, fellas. Let's see what you've got." She sent Phillip a hip bump, which drew chuckles.

Phillip was a master of deadpan. His facial expression remained stolid.

"Our tune: "'S Wonderful." Our topic: The king of fried foods—French fries." Evan stepped back and clustered with Arnold and Robert behind Phillip, who held up their song sheet.

Robert winked at Jane. He was a good sport. Her eyes slid down to take in Darin, playing the song intro, and the memories flooded in.

She'd forgotten the times Darin used to sit at the piano in a little pizza place they had discovered near the college campus. He'd finger the keys, picking out melodies by ear. Sitting shoulder to shoulder, their singing would always attract a group of students who'd join in. Those were good times.

Cecelia nudged Jane. "Bringing back memories with Darin at the piano?"

Jane smiled, "Yeah, he's a talented guy."

Darin pointed to Phillip, and the guys began to sing. Even Robert.

"It's a cinch.
Hunger's quenched.
Fries are real yum-my.
We love fries.
That's no lies.
Best when they're cris-py.
Fries were designed by the French.
Don't be misled by that old mean Grinch.
Oh, it's a cinch.
Hunger's quenched.
And fries are real yumm-my.
We like fries,
and as time flies,
they're best when they're cris-py.
These spuds are not from Italy.
Nor do they come from Germany.
Oh, it's a cinch.
Hunger's quenched.
And fries are real yum-my.
Whoever buys.
We love fries.
And best when they're cris-py!"

The song ended on a high note. Rosemary whooped and everyone stood to applaud. Jane's heart was full. The songs, though silly, for the first time in a long while had lifted her to an unexplained level—above her worries about the future. With the camaraderie and exclamations of crispy fries and onion rings came the belief that God had good plans ahead.

CHAPTER TEN

"Grammys here we come," Evan said and slapped Darin on the back.

Arnold chatted with Phillip, while Robert, digesting the moment of glory, shrunk back into his invisible state. Like experiencing the quick thrill of a Ferris wheel taking you up to great heights, but the ride brings you back down to earth, where you disappear into the bustling crowd.

Robert was the outsider again. But he had picked up another tidbit that could figure into the circumstances related to the cold case. Darin mentioned Martin being known for dalliances. Rhoda had alluded to accepting the hand she was dealt when it came to Martin working with young talent. Had this been his practice eighteen years ago?

The girls joined the boys around the piano. Darin

scooted over and patted the piano bench for Jane to sit next to him.

"You guys were amazing." Jane's smile connected with Robert, and he took it as one of appreciation for participating. Then she turned to Darin. "You haven't lost your piano skills."

"I play less now. Cynthia got custody of the baby grand."

He earned a sympathetic smile from Jane with his wit.

Martin, accompanied by Rhoda, stood on the fireplace hearth and called to them.

"Everyone. Reconvene please. The results are in."

The group moved, separating back into their teams.

"After much deliberation over the songwriting competition, by unanimous vote of the judges, we've arrived at two awards. In the category of Song Most Likely to Be Made into a Broadway Musical," Martin said, "is ... 'The French Fry Song.'"

"If they can produce a musical called 'Hairspray,' one titled 'French Fries' is sure to be a hit," Evan said.

Rhoda waited for the chatter to die down and said, "The Song Most Likely to Be Played at the International Debutante Ball in New York City's Waldorf-Astoria Hotel, is ... 'The Onion Ring Song.' I can see the debutantes doing the Onion Ring and loving it. Good job girls."

"Speaking of onion rings," Evan said, "the spiciest and crunchiest I've ever eaten were at the Heart of

Montgomery Club when I was Darin's guest. You should take the girls there to sing for their supper."

"Sorry. No connections there now, due to …" Darin shot an unfriendly look at Martin, who either didn't hear the comment or chose to ignore it.

What was that about?

Evan wrinkled his forehead and started to speak but Jane filled the uneasy space. "All this food talk and the smells of garlic, tomato and oregano wafting from the kitchen is making me hungry. What's cooking?"

"Another evening of Italian cuisine. Lasagna will come out of the oven shortly," Arnold said.

"And we have garlic bread and salad with Arnold's own blend of red wine vinaigrette dressing," Cecelia added.

The couple who had married so young, impressed Robert as a happy team. They hosted a pleasant dinner, and everyone pitched in to clean up. Phillip started the fire outside so it would be ready for roasting marshmallows, and they gathered in front of the TV, per Jane's instructions.

"Tonight, we view a nostalgic snippet of our lives recorded for posterity."

The group gathered. Robert hung back to let everyone settle. Couples paired. Jane sat in a corner chair beside the television with the controls. Darin took the chair opposite her.

Robert grabbed a stool from the pub table and placed it where he could view everyone. The chair seat, constructed of a natural reed material, furnished homespun appeal but not comfort.

Jane, who had pulled her hair back into a cute, messy ponytail, quieted the group. "We've had fun with two of the Gershwin songs we used to perform but tonight we'll have a blast from the past. My mom purchased the entire video of the tri-county high school concert. So, I have for you … our last performance together."

"Do you furnish tissues?" Arnold asked, and wrapped his arm around Cecelia.

"What about popcorn?" Evan said.

"And drink," Darin added.

Jane held up her hands. "We just ate, guys. We'll do s'more after this."

"'S wonderful," Rosemary blurted and drew laughs.

Jane started the video, and the title covered the screen: *Tri-County High School Chorus Concert, Woodruff Fairgrounds, May 23, 2002.*

The night of the murder.

Robert looked for a reaction from Martin or Rhoda and detected nothing noticeable. An official gave a welcome, center stage. But two things caught Robert's interest. The date and time stamp running in the lower corner of the screen and the positioning of the camera captured not only the stage but the first several rows where students were seated.

A group stood, filing out of the front rows, to take the stage.

"There we go," Evan said.

"And you were still breathing heavy behind me," Jane said to Darin.

"Lusting over her?" Evan winked at Darin.

"No," Jane said, "if you recall, you and Darin came charging in late, still buttoning your shirts. Rosemary and Phillip followed right on your heels. Cece and I were afraid we'd have to sing all the parts by ourselves."

"We were supposed to wear our superior-rating choir pins," Rosemary said. "Phillip took me back home to get mine. He looked out for me, even then," she said, patting Phillip on the shoulder.

Her earlier excuse for their almost being late was because Phillip stopped to clean off his shoes. There was a foot cast taken of a partial shoe print in the dirt at the Singletary house near the point of forced entry.

"Curtain's going up," Caroline pointed.

The time read 8:04. The choral group of about forty students stood on risers. The girls wore black dresses, the boys wore white shirts and black pants. Martin, his back to the audience, also wore a white shirt and black slacks. In front of the risers, stood the ensemble, wearing colorful 1920s outfits.

"The six Valley Voices, the cream of the crop," Martin said.

"Aren't there seven of you? Was someone missing?" Caroline asked.

"Arnold was the cream above us all because he managed the sound and lighting," Evan said. "He had the task of making us look and sound good."

"Those skills were the only way I could hang with the group, 'cause I couldn't sing worth a flip."

"Arnold was tough to replace," Martin said. "Shoot, all of you were hard to replace when you graduated. I wish more of you produced progeny like Cecelia and Arnold. Amy is a new generation of talent."

Amy whisked her long silky strands of hair over her shoulder and turned to smile at Martin. Robert captured the tension in Rhoda's jaw.

"You two surprised us, all right—eloping—" Evan began.

But Arnold pointed to the screen. "Hush. The first song is about to start."

Robert's concern with group analysis and the press of the hard seat beneath him shifted to a fascination with the characters on the screen. Their first song, Robert now knew intimately. They sang "'S Wonderful" with gusto and cute, choreographed body movements.

Jane on video held Robert's attention. She wore a bright yellow dress covered with rows of fringe. A matching yellow headband, wrapped about her forehead, tamed her curls. The fringe of the dress wiggled and flipped about with her moves. She was terrific.

The performance included Rosemary and Phillip singing "Our Love is Here to Stay" to each other, which brought sighs from the group and concluded with "They

Can't Take That Away from Me".

Robert didn't have to be familiar with the song to appreciate the lyrical sentiment of holding onto memories, even though you may not meet again on the bumpy road to love. Did his and Jane's almost relationship fit the lyrics? He blinked, suddenly realizing the clapping from the crowd on the video extended to the room.

"So sweet, Rosemary and Phillip, to think your love really is here to stay after all these years," Cecelia said.

Rosemary hugged Phillip and smiled at her friend. "You and Arnold paved the way."

"We sing again in the finale. Want to watch it?" Jane asked.

"Nah. We've seen the most awesome of the high school groups," Darin said.

"Ooh, you were so good," Caroline said, patting Evan's knee.

"Martin trained our voices, and Rhoda taught us our moves. Did you see us perform that night, Rhoda? We had just learned the shoulder tilt and turn." Evan demonstrated.

Rhoda glanced at Martin. "I … don't think so."

"'S wonderful,'s marvelous, s'mores. The perfect ending. I've seen enough awesomeness," Arnold said. "I say we gather around the fire pit."

Phillip stood and pulled Rosemary up beside him. "The fire should be burned down and the supplies for the s'mores are ready and waiting."

The date and time stamp were frozen on the screen of the paused video. Robert had made another major error in the investigation—not viewing the video of the concert. He could rectify that tonight; he'd make an appearance at the fire pit and look for a good time to excuse himself.

Glancing at the eighteen-year older faces lit by the shadowy light from the TV screen wrought a stark reality. Sometime in the span of that night, when the Valley Voices sang and danced, Veronica Singletary's life was ripped from her. Did someone in this room hold the key to her murder? The sensation bristling his scalp told him the answer was yes.

~

Powering off the video, Jane dabbed at tears triggered by not only the music but the memories of her senior year and close choir friendships. Past hopes and dreams bubbled inside her but, like bubbles, they had burst.

This group of seniors had been like a small family, achieving a closeness she'd lost in her biological family when her parents divorced. Together, the ensemble had experienced great times as well as the trauma of Mrs. Singletary's tragic murder. When one hurt, they all hurt, and Mr. Sing was one of them.

She sometimes wondered if the need to stop the hurt was part of the driving force behind Cecelia and Arnold's hasty marriage. They took hold of life and love while they were able since life could be snatched away at any moment. And now, they had beautiful Amy.

Maybe seeing the concert video and getting to know Mr. Sing better would help Robert remove him from the suspect list.

She'd been neglecting Robert. Not intentionally, but it was simply the way the day had unfolded. She'd remedy his being left out when they gathered around the fire pit.

Giggling and chitchat lightened the mood as they stepped outside.

"We have hand whittled sticks ready for you," Caroline said.

"With nice sharp points. I helped." Rhoda muttered behind Martin, who was laughing and bumping shoulders with Amy as they filed out of the great room onto the terrace.

Dusk had closed in, as if pulling down shades to provide a backdrop for the stars. A cozy fire lapped at the logs. The warmth was pleasant in the cooler night air. The classmates took seats. Four concrete benches formed a circle around the fire pit. Couples grouped.

Jane took Robert's hand to be certain they sat together. Darin took a seat on her other side. She and Darin were friends, just as she and Robert, but guilt niggled her. Though Darin's confession was flattering, she wasn't sure how she felt about his "I never should have let you go" statement. She'd read of romances being rekindled at reunions. Could this be happening to her? She felt a lurch in her chest at his smile. However, the emotion differed little from the feeling she had in her teens, when her missing puppy was returned.

As Rosemary's maid of honor, she'd be paired with Darin, who was best man. But she was here with Robert. She'd try to draw him into the conversation.

"Have you ever made s'mores?"

"Certainly. Any true Boy Scout has s'more making down to an art," Robert said.

Then Caroline spoke up. "I made s'mores with my Brownie troop at the park near the foot of the River Bridge just outside of town. Do y'all know the spot?"

"I do. It's where I proposed to Cecelia."

Cecelia grabbed Arnold's hand. "We refer to River Bridge as the Proposal Place."

"I used to think that was the official name of the bridge," Amy said.

"Start those marshmallows around, Evan." Rosemary grabbed a marshmallow and passed the bag to Rhoda. "Phil and I spent many a night on the banks beneath the bridge, gazing at the stars. Evan, River Bridge is where you used to pick up Phillip and give him a ride to school." Rosemary's marshmallow flamed up. She blew on it and stuck it over another place in the fire. "Back in the days when you looked out for your friends."

Jane wasn't sure if Evan caught the dig, but she did. Rosemary was determined to not let up on Evan for giving Jane's job to Caroline.

When the bag came to Darin, he took out two

marshmallows and poked one on the end of Jane's stick, the other on his. "Here you go, all ready to roast."

She accepted the stick, and Darin passed the bag to Robert.

"You're not going to put a marshmallow on my stick?" Robert asked.

Was he making fun of Darin? Or did he really feel slighted?

"Do you want me to?"

"No, just kidding." There was no hint of humor on his face. The camaraderie was not going as she had planned. Robert placed a marshmallow on his stick and held it over the fire.

Jane did the same. "Robert, what did you think of our concert?"

"I believe your group is very talented. I especially liked the way you made your yellow dress shimmy and shake."

"I was thankful all eyes were on the girls, so us guys with no rhythm went unnoticed," Phillip said.

"Speak for yourself, my friend," Evan said. "My moves were pretty slick."

"So slick he slid and tripped me at a mall performance." Darin pulled his marshmallow out of the fire. "I thought we were going down like dominoes."

"There was a slippery spot on the floor. Besides, I was told my move livened up the performance."

"It livened things up all right," Martin said. "People thought we'd added a comedy routine to the show."

"Jane, your marshmallow is on fire." Darin scooted closer to her, grabbed her stick, and blew out the flame. "You want another one to start over?"

"No. Crusty is good."

Banter continued around the circle, and Robert went silent.

"It's a beautiful, clear sky tonight. You can see the Big Dipper." Jane pointed.

"Perfect conditions to see a shooting star," Martin said.

"I'm going to make a wish," Amy said, looking up at the sky.

"You need to see a shooting star first to wish on it." Arnold patted his daughter's knee.

"On any clear night, it is possible to see between one and two shooting stars per hour. If they come more frequently, it's called a meteor shower." Caroline unpacked her latest bundle of knowledge.

Rosemary jumped up. "If you want to make a wish on a shooting star, you don't have to look far. How about it, SSR girls?"

Ceclia smiled, motioned to Jane, and they stood side by side.

"I probably shouldn't ask, but I will. What is SSR?" Evan asked Rosemary.

Rosemary lifted her chin. "Shooting Stars Rule." She held up her hand, palm out. Jane joined Cecelia in doing the same, and all three recited, "our friendship will shine and rule forever."

"We formed a club in middle school binding us together," Rosemary said. "We have a song, favorite TV show, heartthrobs—all kinds of stuff."

"This I have to hear," Arnold said. "Who were your heartthrobs?"

"Shall we tell, ladies?"

Cecelia looked at Jane and snickered. "I'm not sure I even remember."

"I do," Rosemary said. "From the TV show, *Beverly Hills 90210*," she pressed her hand to her chest, "my pick was Dylan. Cecelia, how could you forget? You adored David."

"Oh, yeah." Cecelia's cheeks pinked up, and she looked at Arnold. "That was before you came on the scene, dear."

Arnold laughed. "Good thing, if you expect me to continue toasting your marshmallow."

"Are you still pining over Dylan?" Phillip asked, nudging Rosemary with his skewer stick.

"I might consider it, if you keep jabbing me." She pouted and rubbed her arm.

"What about Jane?" Darin asked. "Who was her favorite?"

Jane stepped back from the fire. Her flushed face creating enough heat.

"She got all worked up over Brandon." Rosemary added a bit of taunt to his name.

Jane frowned and batted the air at Rosemary. "I didn't get all worked up. I just thought he was cute."

"Brandon, huh? Okay, shooting stars, I've got a wish for you," Darin said, looking at Jane.

"Hold up," Rosemary said, hands on hips, "just so you know. These shooting stars only make wishes, we don't grant them. And we wished to be granted a glimpse of who our future loves would be."

"And how did that work out?" Rhoda asked.

"I saw Arnold for the first time in eighth grade English class. He sat in the front row. I used to study the back of his head," Cecelia said.

Arnold touched the back of his head. "And I worried about what the front of my hair looked like."

"For me," Rosemary said, "I got my glimpse of Phil the first day of our junior year when he rode into the school parking lot like a knight on a white charger."

Phillip shook his head. "I was driving a 1988 white Mercury Capri with a wired-on bumper."

"I'm just tellin' you what I saw." Rosemary shrugged and plopped back on the seat beside him.

"And Jane, what about you?" Evan asked. "Have you seen any glimpses?"

Jane felt her face flush, and it was not just from the heat of the fire. How had the conversation taken this odd turn?

Rosemary frowned. "Evan, don't put her on the spot. Jane may or may not have glimpsed her future love, but for those of you who are still looking I can offer this advice. Wait for someone who knocks your socks off. Who makes you forget about the past and who you used to be? Who understands and accepts you completely? Today. As you are. Who believes not only in the good Lord but in you? Who stands by your side? Who doesn't want anyone else? Wait for someone you can wish upon a star with."

Rosemary fell silent. Jane and everyone sat staring into the crackling remains of the fire.

In the quiet, Jane mulled over Rosemary's words shared from the depths of her heart. She and Phillip had a remarkable relationship. Had their love not weathered the strain of hardships, time, and distance, she would not have acquired the wisdom to deliver such an eloquent speech.

Rosemary reached for Phillip's hand and spoke again. "Look for the one who understands your non-silent silence. Don't settle."

"On that note, I'm going to say good night." Robert set his stick on the table beside the fire pit. "Thank you for the delicious dinner and dessert treat. I haven't had s'mores for many years."

"You are welcome," Cecelia said, and Arnold nodded toward him.

Everyone mumbled their good nights, while Jane touched his arm and walked with him back to the door of the meeting room.

"I'll be needing some items from the trunk. See you first thing in the morning?"

"No problem."

"Good night. I hope you enjoyed the day."

He pressed his lips together and raised his chin. She wasn't sure how to interpret it. He turned and quietly stepped into the shadows of the lodge's common room. Her hopes for having him become a part of the group faded, just as the flames in the fire pit.

CHAPTER ELEVEN

Jane awoke with a start. Her hip, pressed against the firm mattress, ached. Her face sunk into the fluffy pillow, made breathing difficult. She blinked against the darkness, willing her mind to focus on where she was. Her hair carried the scent of smoke. The fire. Roasting marshmallows on the terrace.

Last evening had been pleasant, except Robert had left early, leaving her uneasy. She had hoped he would become more comfortable with her friends and her former teachers. He'd even surprised her by participating in the song writing activity.

She pushed up on her elbows, squinting to focus on the digital clock beside the bed. Five o'clock. Still dark outside. All seemed quiet. After a trip to the bathroom and splashing cool water on her face, she returned to her writing table and snapped on the lamp.

Up before everyone, she'd use this time to let God's soothing spirit lead her. This busy day needed a positive start.

She turned to Psalm 143 and prayed for the words to penetrate her heart and mind with wisdom and insight. When she reached verse ten, she closed her eyes and recited it from memory, savoring the sweet words.

"You are my God. Show me what you want me to do, and let your gentle Spirit lead me in the right path."

This month marked one year since her mother's death from cancer. Over the past year she had managed home repairs to prepare for the sale of her mother's house, mended her relationship with her brother, and learned a whole new career in private investigations with all the rules, and hard to define skills. Robert had been brave to take an elementary school teacher with a bent toward history under his wing and give her on-the-job-training.

But now, her time with Robert was almost over, and what she thought was in her future had changed. Writing all new lesson plans to meet state standards made her head hurt. Not to mention dealing with older students, discipline, and classroom structure—in a pandemic.

And then there was the matter of Evan humiliating her by announcing in front of friends that she'd been replaced. And bringing her replacement with him. Jane wriggled her toes against the coarse mat beneath her feet. Caroline was adorable and smart. But heaven help her, she couldn't avoid relishing the barbs Rosemary shot at Evan every chance she got for giving Jane a raw deal.

Lord, I am in a quandary. Show me the right path.

She rested her head on her arms, folded across her Bible for a moment.

Clanging sounds broke the silence. Was someone in the kitchen? She grabbed her robe, thrust her arms in the sleeves, and zipped it. Her future would have to wait.

Darin was filling a *See Rock City* mug with steaming brew when Jane walked into the kitchen. "You're an early riser."

"I am most days."

The aroma of fresh coffee mixed with sweet scents coming from the oven. "Whatever your baking smells good."

"Baking? I'm making muffins from a package mix."

"If it's not in a wrapper and ready to eat, it counts as baking. I'm impressed."

He flashed his dimples. "Coffee?"

"Yes, thank you." Jane sat on a kitchen stool. The soft glow of the light from under the stove hood cast a cozy domestic ambiance over the early morning scene. Darin slid a ceramic mug in front of her.

"Perfect selection for today's activities."

"The coffee?"

"No, the flowers on this mug. Rosemary wanted her wedding to be a non-extravagant affair by not going into debt with florist flowers and expensive dresses. She insisted I choose a dress I could wear for other occasions and vowed to use wildflowers for the ceremony."

"Rosemary's request must be why Phillip told me to wear a sport coat and khakis instead of renting a tux."

"Right. And finding plant life around here for bouquets, head crowns, and lapels is the morning's order of business."

"You've done an amazing job of organizing the wedding for Rosemary and Phillip."

"I wanted to show our love for them by involving everyone in the wedding preparations. We missed the fun of wedding planning for Cecelia and Arnold when they ran off to get married."

"The reception you threw for them was nice."

"Nice, but still not what we'd promised for each other."

"A Shooting Star promise?" Darin pursed his mouth in a smug smile.

"Yes. And don't make fun."

"I'm not making fun. I think it shows integrity by taking your pledge to one another seriously and living up to it."

With her finger, Jane traced the outline of a flower on her mug. "We promised to make each other's weddings shine."

"Is that why you had Cecelia and Arnold's reception outside under the stars?"

"Rosemary and I talked about making lots of foil covered cardboard stars and using the fellowship hall at my grandmother's church, or clearing out Rosemary's uncle's old hay barn, hanging a mirror ball, and spotlighting it."

"Barn weddings are actually in vogue."

"It was my mother's idea to ask the Valleytown Nursery if we could use their garden, which put us outside under the real stars."

"Ingenious. I always liked your mom. She relocated to Mobile after we graduated?"

"She did. I moved there, too, after her cancer diagnosis."

"You were brave to give up your job to take care of her. Few would do the same—me included, I'm afraid."

Jane shrugged. "It was difficult, but I'm thankful for the last days we shared, before she became really sick. Evan gave me leave so I didn't lose my retirement standing."

"Phillip told me about Evan's indelicate way of telling you he gave Caroline your old job and changed the grade you'd be teaching."

"My degree is Elementary Education, which covers fifth grade, but—"

"You're not pleased about the change."

"Does it show?"

Darin nodded. "But mostly from Rosemary's not-so-subtle digs." He reached out and touched her hand. "I feel I should take the blame."

"What? Why?"

"I talked you into changing your major to education, when your passion was in history."

"You remembered?"

"Of course. I remember everything about you."

"You suggested education, but I'm the one responsible for taking your suggestion. Honestly, reflecting back, you had a good point. Every community in the nation has schools and needs teachers. My focus on history would have limited my job opportunities."

"I'm glad we have some time to talk." He pulled a folded scrap of paper out his wallet and handed it to her.

"What's this?"

"I saw this job listing in the latest Heart of Montgomery newsletter and thought of you."

Under a section titled 'looking for' was a list: hostess, sushi specialist, historian archivist and yoga instructor. Historian archivist was underlined.

He smirked. "They haven't removed me from the mailing list yet. You should apply for the job."

"Evan brought up the Heart of Montgomery last night. If they want a historian, the club has been around a long time?"

"It's a prestigious association started in the late 1800s."

The idea of digging through old photos and newspaper clippings made Jane's hands itch with anticipation. Something about stepping back in time, seeing how others dressed, and what interests occupied their time, invigorated her.

"They are looking for someone to capture the flavor of the past."

A ray of hope flooded over Jane like a soothing balm. "Being an archivist would be a dream job for me, but it wouldn't be wise to give up my eleven years in the state retirement system."

"You'd be able to do something you love and make important contacts. The club pays well, offers health and dental benefits, and has a 401K plan. You could wave bye-bye to elementary school."

Jane leaned back in the chair and let out a sigh. "It's worthwhile just seeing the clipping and knowing the job exists. Thank you for thinking of me." She handed the paper back to Darin.

"No. You keep it." He placed the paper in her palm, lightly closing her fingers over it. "Give it some serious thought. I'd be glad to give you a recommendation."

The oven timer beeped, breaking the spell. Jane took the paper, folded it carefully, and placed it in her robe pocket.

Delicious smells wafted from the oven and the opened door exposed lightly browned muffins peaked to perfection in the muffin tin.

"Nothing like fresh hot muffins." Jane pulled saucers from the cupboard while Darin retrieved butter from the fridge.

In a moment, they settled back at the island. Jane bit into a muffin laced with warm chocolate chips that melted with gooey goodness on her tongue. They clinked mugs in an impromptu toast, celebrating a renewed friendship.

She'd prayed only minutes before for God to lead her in the direction she should go. Was this job suggested by Darin her answer? And was Darin's declaration yesterday further evidence of a new direction for her to consider?

But there was her PI work ... and Robert. Robert had made it clear personal involvement was taboo. Though a kiss on a moonlit night took them by surprise, they'd both agreed to keep things professional. With her moving from Mobile, her work with the agency was on a road with a "dead-end" sign. But she wouldn't mind swapping the sign to "new construction-opening soon."

"If I were to look at a job outside the retirement system, I'd have to consider staying with the investigations agency. Robert has invested time and effort in training me and even given me a badge. I'd have to at least see if he wanted me to stay on at the agency."

"I wasn't going to say anything but since you mentioned him, he's kind of poking around ... and … well, frankly, making us a little uncomfortable."

Jane straightened. "What do you mean, poking around?"

"During the songwriting activity he was asking about

our desire to go to Europe after graduation, and we wondered how he knew about it."

"I had no idea. I mean he worked the murder of Mr. Sing's wife and ... well he was interested in reviewing the old case ... the case was never closed." She was prattling and making things worse. "Your talking about going to Europe may be in the case notes. I'm sure he didn't mean to make you feel uncomfortable. I'll mention it to him. It's getting late. I'd better shower and dress. Thanks for the muffins." She patted her pocket where she had placed the clipping. "And for thinking of me."

She hurried from the kitchen. She'd asked him to be discreet about exploring clues in the cold case. Was he looking at her friends as suspects now? She had to talk to Robert right away.

~

The sitting room at the foot of the stairs offered a cozy setting to wait for Jane, where he could talk to her away from the others. He was surprised she hadn't knocked on his door yet, since she'd mentioned needing to get supplies from the trunk.

Next to the stone fireplace in the windowless room stood a glass front case with a collection of eagle statuary. He reached inside the cabinet and snapped on the display light. The illuminated eagle replica on the top shelf eyed him. Wouldn't it be nice to see into a murder mystery with the acuity of the eagle eye, seeing four to five times greater than a human?

As Jane had requested, several Valleytown High yearbooks rested on the sofa table. One book was open. Evan's picture, the face leaner and hair longer, smiled at him. In the handwriting next to his photo, the word Europe stood out. Robert sat down and took a closer look.

See if your 'rich uncle' comes up with more than 3 one-hundred-dollar bills. No way you're jumping off to Europe without me.

Add three to the one-hundred-dollar bill Phillip said he found, and the answer came to four. The exact amount and same denominations as the cash taken from the Singletary house.

From Martin's statement, the missing money was in hundred-dollar denominations. Martin's comments had seemed scripted when Robert brought up Martin's conversation with his wife about the money.

I would hate to think ... no ... it had to be the break-ins...

But wouldn't ramblings and searching for answers by the husband of a murdered wife be expected? Did Martin have a hidden agenda when he mentioned the students hearing his conversation? Or were the students involved?

The investigative process is a progression of steps moving from evidence gathering tasks to information analysis, theory development and validation leading to sufficient grounds for an arrest and charge of a suspect. Evidence gathering was the job of CSI. His job was to deal with all the other steps, including talking to witnesses and suspects. In this case, he'd done a poor job.

He returned the book to the table and wiped his moist palms against his jeans.

He felt like a filleted fish—his investigative shortcomings lying exposed where he'd mishandled his assignment. The lead officer had relied on him. He was a rookie who had not done a thorough job.

The things left undone glared at him. Top of the list should have been what he did last night—watch the video of the night in question in its entirety. He'd talked to the principal, who corroborated Martin's whereabouts between 6:30 and 9:30 at the time of his wife's murder. Not investigating further had been a grave mistake.

What should he say to Jane*? I believe your friends need to be added to Martin as suspects in the death of Veronica Singletary?*

She knew the rule: Everyone is a suspect until they aren't. Avoiding personal involvement with potential witnesses was another.

Jane was incapable of being objective, because the witnesses were her friends, so it was up to Robert to deal with the troublesome issue. The handwritten note from Darin in Evan's yearbook was a new puzzle piece spinning in his head, along with the others he'd discovered. And he still had to share what he'd found with Jane.

The video revealed the precise timing of what occurred at the concert on that fateful night. After their Gershwin performance, the Valley High choir left the stage at 7:52. Martin stood in the aisle, with Cecelia beside him, as the students filed into their reserved seats.

At 7:55 Cecelia says something to Martin. He frowns, reaches toward her forearm, but she turns and goes out the exit door to her left. Once all the students are seated. Martin takes an outside seat. The group on stage begins singing. Martin leans over, says something to the student on his right, gets up, and goes out the exit door at 7:59. He returns at 9:02.

The Valley High group returns to the stage for the finale, minus Cecelia, at 9:10. An electric charge tingled over his skull. The vibration in his body he had learned to pay attention to.

The students from all the represented choirs had taken their places—five choral groups with five conductors on stage together. The blended voices reached the climactic end, with the choir leaders coaxing voices to hold their notes.

Each director had his own style. One held his hands straight up. Another pushed forward with one hand and held his other hand to his ear. Two others held palms up, as if lifting something heavy. Martin's style was more reserved. With his elbows close to his sides and fingers pinched together, he slowly moved his hands outward horizontally. When he snapped his fingers into fists. The voices stopped. Applause erupted.

In that instant, Robert saw it. He rewound the video, comparing the beginning to the end to be certain. A new piece in the murder puzzle. But where did it fit?

Concrete clues were cropping up. Cecelia and Martin had left during the concert. Females figured into the neighborhood break-ins. Cecelia had opportunity but what about motive?

"Hey man."

Evan startled Robert.

"Glad to see someone else up. Have you heard from any of the girls upstairs?"

"Not a peep. I'm waiting on Jane."

"And I'm waiting on Caroline. Mind if I join you?"

"Not at all." Robert scooted over, making room for Evan. "I hope you don't mind, but your yearbook was open, and I saw the note Darin wrote when you graduated."

"These yearbooks, like that video last night, bring back lots of memories."

"I bet." Robert tapped the slick photo page. "Darin mentions the trip to Europe we were talking about yesterday. He says he hopes your rich uncle might come up with more than three hundred. I take it the trip was a much-discussed mission?"

"Sure. A pipedream. A lot of talk, but the idea fizzled."

"Was the rich uncle a fantasy? You mentioned you and both of your parents were only children."

Evan's grin slid from his face. "What is this?" He moved to the edge of the couch. A vein in his neck twitched. "Why all the questions about money?"

It wouldn't do to tell him he had learned of the cash and uncle remarks from reading Jane's diary.

"What money?" Jane appeared, still in her robe and slippers.

"Where did you come from?" Robert asked.

"I was in the kitchen talking to Darin."

Darin materialized from the shadows of the great room. "You're talking money?"

"He is." Evan pushed up from the couch. "To be specific, he questioned me about the money I received for graduation."

"Why?" Jane asked.

Robert had three sets of eyes on him, waiting for an answer.

"Evan doesn't have an uncle."

"Rich uncle is a colloquialism, a manner of speaking," Evan said, and received an approving nod from Darin. "I thought you were just here as Jane's date."

"He is." Jane crossed her arms and stared at him, perhaps glared was more descriptive.

Phillip walked in from the first-floor hallway.

Rosemary trotted down the stairs. "Mornin' babe." She pecked Phillip on the cheek, then looked at the others. "Why so serious?"

"Is there a problem here?" Phillip asked. "Things sounded tense when I came in."

"The investigator here is concerned that I don't have a rich uncle," Evan said.

Phillip pressed his lips together and frowned. "I don't get it."

"I do," Evan said. "He's implying I stole the money from Mr. Singletary's house." Evan hoisted his hands to his hips. "As improbable as it may seem," he raised his index finger and pointed with dart-like accuracy, "I found those three one-hundred-dollar-bills on the riverbank beside the bridge."

Phillip stepped up. "I was with Evan. And like I told you when you interviewed me, I found a one-hundred-dollar-bill on the landing beside the bridge. I was already on probation for theft when Principal Jones gave me a break and withheld reporting me for stealing money out of drink machines at school. His eyes appeared cold. But your questioning me led to the principal's serious suggestion that I go into the military. If I didn't, he'd turn in the report he'd withheld.

"It's no secret we all heard about the four-hundred-dollars at Mr. Sing's house," Darin said. "You could tag any of us with reasons to want the money, but murder? I, for one, don't appreciate being considered a suspect."

"So, you came here to slip your questions in on us?" Evan looked from Robert to Jane. "You brought him here to spy on us?"

"Of course not," Rosemary said, then cut her eyes to Jane. "Did you?"

CHAPTER TWELVE

Heat flooded Jane's face. She felt as if she'd been punched in the chest. But instead of pain, she found it hard to take a breath ... or think straight. "Spy? Certainly not. Robert was … uh … interested …" Jane stumbled over her words, trying to keep them light. "…since you were all—"

Robert, still seated, held up his hands in surrender. "Sorry. I owe you an apology. I didn't mean to upset everyone. Please don't blame Jane. It's the bane of being an investigator. The inclination to inquire is hard to restrain."

"Shucks." Rosemary reached in front of Evan and jabbed Robert on the knee. "Understandable." She turned to Jane and peered at her through green cat eyeglasses with magnified compassionate eyes. "I'm starved and I need coffee."

"I made coffee and muffins," Darin said.

"I knew you were good for something." Rosemary hooked one arm with Darin and the other with Phillip. "Evan, come on. Caroline said she'd be down in a little bit." The group left.

Jane faced Robert. Every muscle in her body tensed. *What now?* She had to keep going and smooth things over. "I need craft supplies," she said through clenched teeth. "Can I get them?"

Robert stood, said nothing, and walked to his room.

Jane closed the door behind them. She batted the heel of her hand against her forehead. "What were you doing?"

"Waiting on you." Robert walked to the trunk, flipped open the latches and lifted the lid.

"No. Ro…bert." She dragged his name out in a whine, squeezing her eyes shut. "I mean, what were you doing questioning my friends? Darin tells me you asked last night about them wanting to go to Europe."

"I did. Friendly conversation."

"If it was so friendly, why did he take it differently? He claimed you were poking around in their past and made them feel uncomfortable."

"Guilty conscience?"

"You think everybody has some ulterior motive. Darin is my friend."

"You think the guy who dumped you is your friend? I don't trust him."

"That's your trouble. Sometimes people do things

with no hidden agenda. He told me about a historian job at the Heart of Montgomery Club. He feels bad for talking me into changing my major and remembered my love for history."

"That so? Or is he trying to plan your life and you're falling for it again?"

"Like I fell for your assurance that you would keep your investigation tactful? At least he's trying to help me and not attempting to pin a murder on my friends."

What had happened to Robert? The guy she could count on for loyalty and having her back? The one she didn't think she could ever count on again was Darin. But he remembered her interests and had thought enough of her to save a job listing she might be interested in.

Rosemary had said, "Don't settle. Look for the one who understands you and who will stand by your side." She would have put Robert in that category. He understood her. He accepted her as is. He'd kissed her, and she'd kissed him back—a memory she couldn't erase, though they had agreed to try. But now his law enforcement mindset was taking first seat and Darin was filling Rosemary's creed.

"I said I was going to be looking into the murder. I'm simply asking questions to help with the case."

"Help what? Broaden your circle of suspects?"

"I neglected to speak with the ensemble group who heard Martin and Veronica discussing the four-hundred dollars. I can't ignore the opportunity to talk to witnesses when everyone is right here."

Her pulse quickened. "Next thing you'll be accusing me. I would have liked to go to Europe after graduation, and I sure didn't have the money. Or maybe I needed money for college, which I did. Motive and opportunity, right?"

"When *did* you hear about the four-hundred dollars?"

Did he really just ask her that question? She crossed her arms and tapped her foot, her slipper making a muffled noise against the wood floor.

"Not making an arrest on your first murder case has wrinkled your brain. Initially, you narrowed it to Mr. Sing. Now everybody is suspect, including me?"

"Look. I'm sorry for the way things unfolded out there this morning. I was waiting for you. I wanted to talk to you about what I had discovered. But Evan came in. I had seen a note written by Darin in Evan's yearbook mentioning money from his uncle and Europe. I merely asked him how an uncle gave him money if his parents were both only children."

"What happened to discreet? Pointing out he couldn't have an uncle if his parents were only children is not discreet. It's confrontational. Maybe it was a great uncle."

"He already admitted he lied about the uncle. Now he says he found the money—three one-hundred-dollar bills. Phillip also claims he found a one-hundred-dollar bill. Four hundred dollars total—the amount missing in the Singletary case."

Jane's limbs felt like heavy weights. "We are here, foremost, for the wedding and a happy stress-free time. Any delving and whatever discoveries you make—can't you keep under wraps?"

"Are you at all interested in what I discovered?"

Jane flopped down on the bed. The mattress was soft and puffed around her hips. But their conversation was far from soft. She closed her eyes. "You might as well tell me."

I watched the entire video of the chorus presentation. Both Martin and Cecelia left the concert. Cecelia can be seen saying something to Martin. She left and did not return."

"Yes, because she was feeling nauseous and went home sick."

"Martin left exactly four minutes later and returned in a little over an hour for the finale."

"He could have been helping backstage."

"He went out the exit door."

"Is that it?"

"No. When Martin returned, he had on a different shirt."

"But ... how do you know?"

"The shirt he wore before he left had button cuffs. When he returned, he was wearing a shirt with cuff links."

"Maybe he got coffee and spilled it and had to change."

"And wouldn't he go home to change his shirt?"

"Oh … I see where you're going with this. But maybe he had a change of shirts he kept in his car."

"And maybe your reactions prove my point that being personally involved affects objectivity."

"Objective is stating facts. Cecelia was sick. And Mr. Sing's change of shirt could be explained."

"You commented last night about how Darin, Evan, Rosemary and Phillip arrived late, barely making it before you went on stage. Lies coupled with motive and opportunity mean something and must be analyzed. Inconsistencies and little things matter. You can't put your head in the sand and decide in advance who didn't do it. And I was wrong to decide in advance who I thought committed the crime." Robert raked his hands through his hair and paced. "Your thoughts are skewed."

Jane sat upright. "Mine are skewed? Yours are warped. Are you saying my friends broke into Mr. Singletary's house, stole the money, and murdered his wife so she wouldn't tell?"

"You have to look beyond middle schoolers who made pledges and pined away over secret television loves and guys in high school who had peepholes into the girl's showers."

"Where did you hear about peepholes?"

Robert stopped his pacing. He was searching for an answer. She could see it on his face. He glanced at the diary sitting on top of the florist wire, ribbon, and other supplies. Jane jabbed an accusatory finger at Robert's chest. "You read my diary. How could you?"

He sighed heavily and sat down on a chair next to the bed. "I did look at your diary, but only those dates around the time of the murder."

"Looks to me like you're grasping for information to create a solution to a murder case that you couldn't solve. What happened to the theory that the murder was related to the neighborhood break-ins?"

"The theory remains. But new information has to be considered. It's the whole point in finding the solution to a cold case."

"Are you so determined to recover your cop image you'll drum up new suspects, no matter who it hurts?"

~

Jane might as well have slammed the trunk lid on his head.

Did she think that little of him? Did she believe he'd formulate facts and dress them up as clues to make himself look good? Or worse, was he guilty of her accusations? Robert opened his mouth, then closed it and shook his head.

"Sorry, that was uncalled for." Jane locked eyes with him.

He held her gaze. "No, you have a point." He couldn't deny it. The idea of solving this case and restoring his reputation as a competent lawman had crossed his mind. "Maybe my motives aren't pure."

What had happened to their easy flow of ideas when

they worked a case? When important facts emerged, they had a system that had evolved. Nothing planned. The method flowed naturally. One hit on an idea and the other made a return with another idea, back and forth, like volleys in a ping pong match. They'd continue to analyze motive and opportunity of all suspects until the right one surfaced. When their investigation aim solidified into a rhythm, they worked together like a well-matched lock and key. But this wasn't one of those times. He was alone in the Singletary matter.

"Can't you turn off your investigator side and just relax? I can't have you interrogating everybody. Can't you see you're ruining things?"

He offered a bitter smile.

She was not the only one personally involved. He was here as her non-boyfriend guest. But Darin's "thoughtfulness" in thinking of a job for Jane bugged him and made him realize there was more to his feelings about Jane than he'd been willing to admit to himself. He'd kissed her and, try as he might, he couldn't help being drawn to her. Add his attempt to work this case, and the combination was like trying to mix gas and water. It didn't work.

These were Jane's friends. He had no right to judge or interfere with her relationships. She was angry and hurt and had every right to be.

But he couldn't fight him not liking her old boyfriends and how they had treated her in the past and in the present. Maybe Evan's reassigning Jane's teaching grade was necessary, but the way he told her was inexcusable. And Darin was crafty. He'd said he had forgotten about Jane's interest in history after Robert brought it up during their songwriting activity. But he apparently latched onto the reminder and used it to his advantage. Smart move, tying Robert's hands.

Vance had emailed the form for the curator job as promised. Now telling Jane he'd requested the application would seem like a ploy. She could interpret his action as trying to take away from Darin's good deed and/or as an attempt to keep her from being upset with him.

Admit it. His pointing out Darin dropping Jane in the past was sheer jealousy on his part. Protecting and shielding Jane from hurt was a task he'd grown accustomed to and one he was going to hate giving up. He had stepped into the center of this debacle, like a spectator stepping over the ropes and into the boxer's ring. He needed to back off and return to the spectator seats, or maybe leave the event all together.

"I thought I could do this—come and play decoy boyfriend and suppress my inner nosy. But I can't turn off analyzing people and their motives. The cop in me is too ingrained. I'm sorry. I'll leave if you want me to."

"Of course not." Jane worried the edge of the throw rug beside the bed with her slipper. "I don't want you to leave. How would I get home?"

"Darin."

"Don't be silly. He lives in Montgomery."

The titter of laughter outside his room told him Caroline had made it downstairs.

"Listen. The last thing I want to do is mess things up for you. I'll be a good boy." He reached for his Louis L'Amour paperback. "I'll read my book and stay out of your hair." He hadn't had breakfast and his stomach grumbled at the sight of the title, *The Trail to Peach Meadow Canyon*. When they'd stopped for the Chilton County peaches, all had been well, but two days later smooth going seemed out of reach.

"I don't want you cooped up in here. I'd like for you to be a part of things."

Robert blew air from puffed up cheeks, slapped his hands against his thighs and stood. "Tell me what you need."

She looked up at him like a dog that bit his master and wasn't sure what to do.

"You needn't look at me with puppy eyes. I have a copy of your schedule." He pulled one from the stack of material in the trunk and dangled it in front of her and forced a grin onto his face. "How can I help with the nature craft?"

A smile crossed over her face, like the sun emerging from behind a dark cloud.

"Truce?"

"I'm running up my white flag, taking off my investigator hat and shall be your non-boyfriend until you get Rosemary and Phillip married off. If I were a Shooting Star, I'd give you the handshake."

"Your desire to give the Shooting Star handshake will have to suffice. Because," she squinted her eyes, "you don't qualify for Shooting Star status."

The old Jane was back. But the jarring hurt of her words—*you're so determined to recover your cop image you'll drum up new suspects, no matter who it hurts*—remained.

CHAPTER THIRTEEN

Jane gave Robert two assignments. The first took him to the woods in search of vines to make floral crowns.

The others had already hit the trail in search of flowers and foliage.

Making his way past the woodshed, twigs snapped beneath his feet, which sent a tiny bird chirping and flitting out of the bushes. If Caroline was with him, she undoubtedly could identify the little brown-feathered creature. But she had decided she could handle flower picking in her flats.

The glint of sunlight from the glass roof of the greenhouse spotlighted a patch of woods to explore. He entered a shady circle of conifers with plenty of wild vine weaving through the underbrush. He breathed in deeply. The air smelled fresh, freeing him from the tensions of the confrontation inside the lodge. Amid the scent of pine mixed with the soothing musk of damp leaves and fallen trees, he pictured himself communing with the Lord in nature's family room.

Considering where to begin with the vine cutting, Robert plucked a pine needle from the ground and poked it between his teeth. The woody flavor was more enjoyable than his hurried breakfast of toast and juice, interrupted by Martin.

"I heard about you questioning Evan. A little late, aren't you?"

"Perhaps. Sometimes information seems worthless, but turns out to be useful."

"Why stir up trouble now?"

"You call continuing to try to apprehend the person responsible for your wife's murder, stirring up trouble? Her case remains open."

Martin cocked his head and forced a smile. "Poor choice of words. It's just … I've had to move on, and some things are best to let go." He glanced toward his former students who were congregating on the terrace. "The money is long gone and untraceable anyhow."

He did it again—insinuation by a quick look at those gathering for the nature walk. His remark appeared to not want to get anyone in trouble, yet the gesture insinuated the students might be guilty of wrongdoing. His hint-dropping had made Robert suspicious of Martin from the outset. Maybe he believed a student was guilty of theft, at least. Or was he just the kind of person who felt compelled to cast blame and instigate rumors?

Of course, the return of the money was not the issue, discovering motive and opportunity were. However, with his promise to Jane, he would let it lie … for now.

After cutting lengths of tough vine with his pocketknife, Robert returned to the terrace where Rhoda had stayed behind, avoiding bees.

Handing her the cuttings, Robert said, “I thought flower crowns were the stuff of Greek mythology and wood nymphs who frolic in the woodlands.”

Rhoda smiled. “Wearing a crown of flowers has a history in the Olympics. A crown of olive leaves went to the victor.”

“Maybe the circle of flowers reflects the victory of the bride getting her man.”

“A stretch.” She clenched her jaw and plunged the vines into the bucket of water used to soak the skewers and held them down. Then slowly releasing her grip, she said, “Flower crowns are trendy. I made one for our daughter to wear with her flower girl dress in my cousin’s wedding.”

Would it betray his promise to Jane if he asked about Martin and Rhoda’s daughter? Discussing children was normal conversation. Right? Besides, Rhoda brought her up.

“I heard your husband say earlier you have a daughter.”

“Breanna. She just finished her first year at Auburn

University."

"You don't look old enough to have one in college."

"She has a December birthday, so is younger than most first year college students."

December. Robert did the math. The school secretary said Martin and Rhoda married in July. If the baby were full term and Martin said she had well-developed lungs, Rhoda would have been two months pregnant when Veronica was murdered.

"Did Breanna follow in your footsteps of music and dance?"

"Her father was disappointed, but she prefers health science to singing. She wants to go to nursing school."

"How about you? Were you disappointed?"

She shrugged. "I want her to follow her passion." She grabbed another piece of grapevine. Her face and neck muscles tightened as she shoved the strip into the bucket of water. "Goodness knows, her father follows his passions."

"Following your interests is a good thing. It's tough to end up in a job you are not well-suited for or don't enjoy."

"You make choices and have to live with them." She pressed the woody branches down vigorously, sloshing water onto the concrete terrace. She gave the impression she'd like to drown some of her choices.

The second assignment Jane gave Robert was to prep the makings for a sub sandwich lunch. The afternoon crafting activity would include DIY sandwiches along with creating boutonnieres, bouquets, and the floral hair garlands.

Rhoda shredded lettuce while Robert sliced tomatoes and placed them on a tray.

"I've attended many weddings, but never provided the flowers for the wedding party," Rhoda said. "Jane has put a lot of work into this wedding for Rosemary and Phillip."

"She had to deal with the pandemic restrictions too."

"Staying isolated and decorating ourselves is a brilliant idea. You must be pleased to have someone as thorough as Jane working for you."

"I'm learning to appreciate her more and more every day."

"Hmm. Any romantic interest?"

Robert mulled over how to respond. His answer had multiple possibilities—No, I see her strictly as an employee who is temporary until she returns to teaching; or I'd love to shower her face with kisses and tell her of my undying love; or I'm a decoy, to make old boyfriends flock around; or I'm here on the pretense of looking like a boyfriend who is really not a boyfriend. He went with a noncommittal statement, with a hint of something more. "We're friends. At least for now."

Rhoda returned a smug grin. "So, you'd probably like to know more about the fellows in her past?"

"It helps to learn about a person's past to understand the present."

"Is that investigator speak?" She used air quotes for emphasis. "Why don't you slice these sub rolls?" Rhoda pushed the bread in his direction. "I'll get out meat and cheese." She went to the refrigerator and returned to the counter. "I think Evan and Darin were friends who both had their eyes on Jane in high school but to get along it seemed they had a system. When one had another girlfriend, the other dated Jane and vice versa."

"Jane was their 'go-to' date when they weren't romancing someone else?" With those guys in her life, it's no wonder she'd feel second-rate. "She dated Darin when she was in college, and he ended up marrying someone else."

"Cynthia Hightower. She was a high-society girl with a law degree from Cumberland in Montgomery. Her father was a bank president and prominent leader." Rhoda opened a glass fronted dish cabinet door and pulled out a platter. "Being a son-in-law gave Darin gold member status in the prestigious Heart of Montgomery Club because Mr. Hightower's father was a founding member. Membership fees come in at twelve thousand … and that's a year. Darin lost his membership when he and Cynthia divorced."

"Sounds like royals losing titles when they step out of line."

"Something like that." She peeled wrappers from cheese slices and circled them around the meat in a geometric display. "I have this information because

Martin became a member through his former wife's family who ran in the same circles. He retained membership since his marriage ended by death and not divorce."

"You live in Montgomery?"

"No, a small town about thirty miles east of Montgomery. But Martin is still involved with the club. Trust me if you're fortunate enough to be grandfathered into the club by a lifetime member, it's worth much more than money." Rhoda snapped a long sheet of clear plastic wrap from a roll and spread it over the platter of meat and cheese, stretching it taut. "Prestige, respect and valuable networking is involved. You can't get it anywhere else."

"What if Jane and Darin got together, and she took a job as club historian, would that give them membership status?"

"Family membership is a perk for administrative employees. But I thought Jane was returning to teaching in the fall."

"She is a history buff, and said Darin mentioned the job to her."

Rhoda sniffed. "Of course, he would."

Rhoda didn't trust Darin either. He didn't want Jane to be hurt. But he dared not mention it. Jane was convinced Robert was sticking his nose where he shouldn't, and she was right. His suspicions could be wrong ... but not likely.

"Hey guys. We're back," Jane said, walking into the

kitchen. “I saw the vines soaking. Thank you.”

“You are welcome,” Rhoda said. “Meats and cheeses are ready.”

“I’m working on the lettuce and tomato,” Robert said. “The sub sandwich assignment is under control. How was the plant life search?”

Jane paused and sucked in air. When she exhaled, her smile appeared more like a grimace. “Good, good.” She laughed; the expression strained. “We have more than enough material to work with.”

Robert had been around Jane long enough to know the sound coming from her was tinged with tense nerves, not relaxed joy. Something had happened out on the trails.

The afternoon craft event went smoothly. Sandwiches were eaten. The girls set up shop in the gaming area to work on the head wreaths.

Jane picked up a twig and a red flower and showed the men how to make boutonnieres by twirling floral tape around the two stems, then tacking on a long pearl topped straight pin.

“Why does yours look better than mine?” Darin’s creation fell apart when he held it up.

Feigning klutziness. An old trick, but it worked. Robert grimace but held his tongue.

Jane pressed in close to Darin and took his hands. “You hold it tight, like this.” She forced his fingers with hers to make the bundle hold together.

"I like this 'holding tight' stuff. I don't think I quite have it. Can you show me again?"

Jane straightened and bumped Darin's shoulder with the heel of her hand. "Darin, you have to do it yourself to get the feel of it."

"Precisely. I'm going for 'the feel of it.'"

When Robert wrote the follow-up cold case report, Darin would qualify for the label of sleazebag on his witness summary.

"Look out now. The Romeo in you is oozing out, and it's kind of sappy," Phillip said.

"Sappy," Evan chuckled. "Oozing out. Good one, Phil."

Robert clenched his teeth, pinched the neck of the boutonniere, and jabbed in the straight pin.

Jane reached across the table and held it up. "Now here is a prototype to follow, boys."

His accomplishment received a pat on the back from both Arnold and Evan seated on either side of him.

Darin nudged Jane with his second attempt. "What do you think of mine now?"

Jane handed Robert's flower back to him. She held up Darin's specimen and patted his shoulder. "A boutonniere maker to emulate."

Emulate?

Emulate the guy who made Jane change her major to something she didn't really like?

The guy who replaced Jane with the socialite who was his ticket into an elitist club?

The guy who was bumped out of the club and was now trying to warm up to Jane to get back in?

Darin was going to force Robert to ask the good Lord for forgiveness for his evil thoughts.

~

"Time for rehearsal," Jane announced.

Robert had helped place the floral projects in the outside refrigerator and returned to the meeting room as an observer.

Martin, at the piano, played a lively tune.

Rosemary let out a "Whoop, whoop." She adjusted her green-winged specs and tapped her toes in a jig to the music.

Robert enjoyed watching the expression of the big military man turn to mush at the sight of her.

When Martin finished playing, Rosemary flopped on a couch next to Phillip. "I'm ready for instructions."

"The wedding will be at sunrise, which is 5:33 a.m. The bachelorette and bachelor parties should end in time for everyone to get some sleep. You need to be up and dressed by 5:00. The wedding will begin at 5:15, during morning twilight."

"Why not marry them off now and then have the bachelor/bachelorette parties," Evan said.

"Think about it, buddy." Arnold poked Evan. "If Phil is married, he's no longer a bachelor. Consequently—no party."

Caroline clasped her hands. "The morning sun peeking over the mountain and shining down on them is going to be enchanting."

Evan shook his head. "I may never know, if I fall asleep."

"What was your wedding like, Mom and Dad?" Amy asked.

"We eloped," Arnold said and wrapped his arm around Cecelia, "but these ladies gave us a spectacular reception."

Rosemary hugged Amy. "We made them restate their vows for good measure."

"The reception tomorrow will be in sunlight instead of starlight," Jane said.

"Then …" Rosemary twirled her finger in circles and pointed to the front door, "you guys scoot."

"First time I ever heard of the honeymooners staying behind and waving goodbye to the wedding attendees," Darin said.

"In a COVID-19 world, we're seeing a lot of innovations."

Jane walked everyone through their paces on the outside terrace. Arnold gave instructions regarding the marriage vows. During the practice recessional, Rosemary blew kisses to her adoring classmates. Then she jumped up, flung her arms around Phillip's neck, and wrapped her legs around his middle.

Phillip, who Robert decided had innards of steel, only staggered back a step. If someone leaped and straddled Robert that way, they'd both crash to the concrete.

Dinner delivery brought everyone inside. Robert was sandwiched between Jane and Evan in the food line, with Rosemary across from them.

"Pizza, fruit and veggie tray, and brownies. Jane, you've done a fantastic job of putting together all the wedding activities," Evan said.

"Another proof of your not so brightness, Evan." Rosemary pulled a piece of pizza loose and plopped it on her plate. "You should have thought of that before giving away her job."

"Administrators have to make tough decisions, and this was one of them."

"As long as you've known Jane," Rosemary pointed a carrot stick at Evan, "how was that a tough decision?"

Robert admired Rosemary's gumption.

"She is a seasoned teacher who I felt could handle the older students better."

"Stop talking about me as if I weren't standing here. Let's keep this a wedding celebration and not a career assessment. Please."

Darin, sitting with Caroline at a pub table for four, called out, "Jane, Evan, over here."

Jane turned and gave Robert questioning look.

"No problem. Go ahead."

"Yeah, Jane, go ahead. I've been wanting to get to know this guy better." Rosemary nudged Robert's shoulder. "Join me and Phil by the fireplace."

The group had split into clusters. Robert listened as Rosemary entertained him and Phillip with her rendition of the morning hunt for flowers. Cecelia, Arnold, and Amy chatted at a table in the library corner. Martin and Rhoda were deep in conversation near the piano.

Robert glanced at the foursome where Jane sat. She may leave her job with him at the agency, but he didn't want her to settle for either of those guys. He hated to see her go back to work with Evan, who didn't appreciate her. And Darin's intentions were underhanded.

Phillip chuckled and Robert turned to see Rosemary mimic stumbling down an incline, trying to reach a flower she had targeted for her bouquet.

With pizza and brownies devoured, the group gathered with coffees. Jane and her chorus teacher stood.

"Mr. Singletary—" Jane began.

Her teacher shook his head. "Martin."

Jane started over. "Martin will share the song he and Amy worked on in summer camp." Jane sat down, and Martin took over.

"Summer music camp allows for more than voice lessons. We work on diction and presentation. Rhoda works out the choreography and I work on expression. When we decided to come to Rosemary and Phillip's wedding, the students at camp had just learned the show tune "Our Love is Here to Stay," which our bride and groom sang so sweetly on the video last night."

"Hear, hear." Darin held up his coffee mug in a toast,

and everyone clapped

Rosemary made a show of bowing.

Phillip smirked and shrugged.

Martin took back control. "It was George Gershwin's final song, composed for The Goldwyn Follies shortly before he died of a brain tumor in 1937, at the age of thirty-eight. The ballad proclaims a love more durable than mountains and boulders." He made a sweeping motion toward the outside landscape. "Like those we've climbed at Eaglemont."

He paused and smiled, his eyes scanned the room, resting on Amy an instant longer than the others.

Seeing this man display his compelling charm gave Robert a sense of how he drew strong reactions. The result might range from devotion to disdain.

"Ira Gershwin, George's brother, wrote the lyrics to this poignant music after George's death, giving the song a special poignancy. It reached some popularity in the 1930s and 40s but when Gene Kelly performed the song with Leslie Caron in *An American in Paris,* the tune became an industry standard."

"And now, Amy and I have worked on a special presentation as a tribute to the bride and groom. Here is our version of "Our Love is Here to Stay."" Martin held out his hand. "Amy."

Amy rose and took a position beside him.

Robert was struck with her poise and posture—her expression reticent, as though they were not present. Robert glanced at Cecelia and Arnold for their reaction.

Arnold's head lifted in pride. Cecelia's lips were pressed together, probably nervous for her daughter.

Martin touched the screen on his phone, perched on the piano. The music began.

Sitting casually on the piano bench, Martin clasped his hands around one knee with the ankle propped on the other knee. He crooned, "It's very clear…"

Amy, chin up, focused on some point behind them.

Uncrossing his legs, Martin continued the song. Amy turned toward him as he sang of passing interests that might fade. Martin stepped closer and took Amy's hand.

Amy took his other hand and her voice sent chills over Robert as she sang that their love was here to stay.

Robert was no music critic, but he could tell she had an exceptional voice. Coupled with her smile and gaze into Martin's eyes, she also did an exceptional job of portraying being in love.

Cheeks touching, they turned to face the group, and both sang about their love going a long way. Clasping hands they continued singing to each other. Martin twirled Amy around and then brought her close to him. They sang with lips only a breath away, then melded into an embrace at song's end.

Robert had little experience in watching romantic acting, but Martin and Amy's performance came across as authentic.

Rosemary jumped up, clapping. Others joined in. But not Cecelia. Or Rhoda.

Cecelia's knuckles went white, fisted in on her knees.

Rhoda sat stoic, feet planted on the floor.

"You two were amazing," Caroline said.

"Rhoda, you toned down the affectionate stuff in high school," Darin said. "But you've got them ready for Broadway."

"So it seems," Rhoda said.

Rosemary crooked her elbow with Amy's and walked with her to join Cecelia and Arnold. "How about our girl? Wasn't she something?"

"Yes." Arnold looked at Cecelia, who said nothing. He cleared his throat. "Really something."

Rosemary patted Amy's hand. "Girl, you got your mama's voice. No offense Arnold."

Arnold gave Amy a shoulder hug. "Good job."

Rosemary reached out for Phillip's hand. "Who would have thought eighteen years ago that Cece and Phil would have a daughter performing that song for us."

Phillip gave a thumbs up, then turned with Rosemary toward Martin. "Mr. Sing, thank you. You took us on a walk down memory lane."

But judging from Cecelia's and Rhoda's reactions, the lane was more like a rat hole.

CHAPTER FOURTEEN

Jane pulled a baggie holding her chorus pin out of the trunk. She glanced at Robert, propped up with pillows on his bed, hands behind his head.

"What's with the fancy pin?"

"The Valley Voices were awarded special pins for earning the highest rating in state competition. She took the pin from the bag and held it for Robert to see up close.

"I am impressed. Are those real diamonds?"

"Real rhinestones that shine like diamonds." She smirked and poked the pin back in the bag. "Cecelia and I agreed to bring our pins for Rosemary to carry in her bouquet as something old."

"Another wedding tradition? I don't see Rosemary as very traditional."

"So much has been modified with coronavirus

limitations, I want to provide as much tradition as possible for her." Jane grabbed a roll of blue satin ribbon from the trunk, tapped the lid, and let it drop with a *thud.*

"A bachelorette party requires craft supplies?"

"Yes, but what I really need is peace of mind at the bachelorette party. What did you think of Amy and Martin's performance?"

Robert unlocked his hands behind his head and let his arms drop to his sides. "You want my thoughts on their vocal ability?"

"No." Jane sat on the trunk lid and frowned. The pizza was not sitting well on her stomach. "The way they presented the song."

"I think either they are great actors or there's something going on between them."

A twinge of nausea struck. "Robert, I saw them together on the trail today. Everyone had scattered to look for flowers or foliage. I took a side path into a hollow and heard voices. I saw a couple partially concealed behind a rock outcropping locked in an embrace. At first, I thought it was Phil and Rosemary who had stolen away for a little quiet time together, so I remained quiet. The male voice said, 'I've been waiting to get you alone.' It was Martin. I was puzzled. Rhoda was back at the lodge. The girl had on black leggings and a pink T-shirt. It was Amy. I'm assuming there was kissing going on. All I could see were his hands running low—way low—down her back, tugging her close. She's only seventeen, and he's forty something and married. Aren't there laws against such things?"

"In Alabama, the age of consent is sixteen, but there is a law against teachers having sex with students under nineteen, if it's gone that far. It's considered an abuse of power from someone students should trust."

Robert's textbook answer made Jane queasier. "I noticed a bit of handholding and Martin touching her back along the trail on our hike yesterday. I wish I could see their choreographed singing as pretend but not after what I saw this morning."

Robert shrugged. "Maybe he got her alone to practice."

"Somehow I don't believe Rhoda choreographed the song with that intensity."

"Your teacher is playing with fire and treading dangerous ground from the expression on Cecelia's and Rhoda's face during their performance."

"That's what I'm afraid of."

"I've worked murder cases over less."

She turned to Robert, her pulse pounding at her temples. "What can we do?"

"Nothing, right now. At least the boys and girls are separated tonight."

"What do the guys have planned?"

"A showing of *Live Free or Die Hard*, an apparent favorite of the groom."

"Go and pal around and let them see you're not their enemy."

"You think watching a movie with stuff getting blown up will make us chums? They'll be comfier if I stay in my room." He held up the book on his nightstand. "And I may finally get a chance to read."

"Whatever you think best." Jane gathered the ribbon and chorus pin. "I need to get back upstairs."

"You might use that ribbon to tie the girl down."

Jane unwound a strip of ribbon and held it up, narrowing her eyes. "A thought."

~

Rosemary's suite bustled with activity when Jane returned with Rosemary's wedding bouquet from the downstairs refrigerator.

Cecelia, Amy, Caroline, and Rosemary had clustered in the tiny kitchen, producing tangy smells. Popcorn kernels pinged in the microwave; nacho cheese warmed on the stove.

"Back up, ladies, and brace yourself for instant delicious, slaved over by yours truly with a knife and handy pre-made roll of dough." Rosemary opened the oven door and the aroma of fresh baked chocolate chip cookies tickled Jane's nose.

"We won't lack for snacks," Amy said, pulling a puffed popcorn packet from the microwave.

"Sweet and salty," Cecelia held up a bag of nacho chips and a bag of Hershey's Kisses, "the evening fare."

"The two flavors match the bride and groom favorites—sweet honey buns and salty peanuts—in our welcome bags," Caroline said.

"Jane's idea." Rosemary nodded toward Jane but sent a smile to Caroline, "Good observation."

Rosemary was dedicated to promoting Jane to Caroline, but Jane was glad to see Rosemary soften her attitude.

Rhoda walked in behind Jane. "Can I help?"

"Yes. I need a spot for us to work on Rosemary's bouquet."

"The big square table in the sitting room?"

"Perfect."

While the others continued with snack preparation, Rhoda helped clear the table to place supplies for working on the bouquet.

"I heard Darin told you about the historian archivist job at the Heart of Montgomery Club."

"Yes, he did."

"Did he also tell you a perk to the job is membership for the immediate family? Unless you're associated with an original founder with lifetime membership or an administrative employee, you must be voted in, and the fee is twelve thousand a year."

"That's a hefty benefit."

"Yes. I'm surprised he didn't mention it."

Rhoda's zinger hit its target. Darin's nice deed wasn't altruism alone. There was a benefit for him attached. A twelve-thousand-dollar benefit. Jane should have known. Darin hadn't changed. He'd just gotten older.

"Thanks for the information."

Rhoda shrugged. "I thought you might like to know."

Jane dusted her hands together. What she thought might be an open door had just slammed shut and Darin's fingers were caught in it.

With snacks on hold, the ladies gathered in the sitting room around the coffee table to listen to Jane's instructions. "We are slated for a movie and snack fun night. Then off to bed. Four in the morning comes mighty early."

Rosemary twirled about like a top. "I won't sleep at all."

"At least rest for now." Jane guided Rosemary to a seat where she flopped like a rag doll.

"First, we'll complete Rosemary's wedding bouquet. I'm passing around this ribbon and scissors. Each of you cut off a piece of ribbon and tie it to the base of the flowers to represent something blue, Cecelia and I agreed to attach our state champ chorus pins for something old."

Cecelia pulled her pin from her pocket. "I practically wore my pin out our senior year. Mine is missing a stone, so it definitely counts as old." Cecelia cut a piece of ribbon, tied it to the base of the bouquet, and attached the pin.

"Something new will be the fresh flowers," Jane said. "What can be borrowed?"

Caroline raised her hand. "Borrow my ring."

Caroline slid it from her finger. Holding it up, multicolored stones glinted in the lamplight. "It was my grandmother's. I can tie it to my piece of ribbon."

Rosemary swallowed hard and reached over to touch Caroline's hand. "You are so kind." She sniffed. "You guys are making me cry and my eyes will be all puffy in the morning."

Rhoda snipped off a piece of ribbon and set the roll and scissors back on the table rather than passing them to Amy, who was sitting beside her. "I'm adding my good wishes with this ribbon," she said, tying the piece of blue satin at the base of the flowers. "And I must add my apologies and forgo the movie. I feel a headache coming on. I can usually ward it off with rest."

"No apologies necessary," Rosemary said, and gave her a hug before she left the room.

Once the ribbon project was complete, Jane placed the bouquet fashioned with dandelions, black-eyed Susans, fern and sprigs of greenery in the refrigerator to keep the flowers fresh. Amy finished making the popcorn and snacks were placed in easy to reach bowls.

Jane cued up the video. "Find your seats, ladies. To fully understand the meaning behind this movie, I must tell you a story."

"Long ago in a little city called Valleytown, lived a girl named Rosemary whose heartthrobs moved from Justin Timberlake to Leonardo Di Caprio and Luke Perry, aka Dylan. One day, Phillip Randolph arrived in town."

Rosemary jumped up. "The boy was hot." She touched her finger to the table and made a sizzling sound … "Yowch." She jerked back, then plopped back in her seat and motioned to Jane. "Sorry, go ahead with your story."

Jane rolled her eyes, and the other girls giggled. "The two became an item in high school but life—the Air Force to be exact—whisked Phillip away."

"Rosemary remained in Valleytown to run her family's downtown eatery. One day a guy, hoping to steal Rosemary's heart, enticed her to the altar. But before the I dos—"

"The girl said, 'I don't,' and bolted." Rosemary flicked her thumb.

Jane had to laugh at Rosemary. "Who's telling this story?"

Rosemary flapped her hands at Jane. "You are. Go on."

"Instead, the hometown girl waited for her true love to return."

"Amen, sister."

Cecelia, Amy, and Caroline applauded as Rosemary took a bow.

"And so, I believe the movie, *Runaway Bride*, is appropriate before you finally say your 'I dos' with the right guy."

"Bring it on." Rosemary settled back into her chair.

Jane dimmed the lights and started the movie. "Enjoy. I'll get bottled water to go with the snacks."

Jane went to the kitchenette. On the counter next to the microwave, lay Amy's cell phone, recognizable in its chartreuse case. As Jane opened the refrigerator door, the phone beeped with a message.

Hang etiquette and pondering invasion of privacy. Jane opened the messages. Her stomach flipped. The very thing she feared. A message from Martin:

Meet me behind the greenhouse, twenty minutes.

Cecelia walked in. "Need help?"

Jane dropped the phone, wishing she could hide it. Too late.

Cecelia talked as she scooped up the phone. "Amy has no pockets in her leggings. She leaves her phone lying—" Her eyes took in the message. Her face lost color and her lips trembled. She jammed the phone in her pocket.

"See that Amy stays here." Cecelia whirled around and stalked out of the suite.

A chill ran over Jane, and it wasn't from the open refrigerator door. She stared at Rosemary's bridal bouquet and the hole with the missing rhinestone on the chorus pin stared back. A cavernous, yawning hole.

The crime report had stated: *A rhinestone and broken fingernail were found in smashed peaches beneath the victim.*

~

Robert was disappointed with himself and, if honest, with Jane as well. He thought Jane was interested in finding the truth. But what did he expect? She was moving back to Valleytown in two months. She would naturally want to have good relationships and be in good standing with her friends. At least she saw her teacher was not golden. And Darin cozying up to her. Couldn't she see he was playing her? Or maybe she did see and was choosing to overlook his ruse.

Let them have their wedding. He'd keep his nose out of the cold case—for now—and his mind off Darin turning Jane's head with a job. *Read your book and forget you care about old flames and rekindled fires.*

Louis L'Amour's cowboy heroes knew how to start a fire. A stone and friction. There'd been friction with Jane when she got mad about him questioning Evan, producing fire—angry fire. The presentation by Martin with Amy exhibited fire—passionate fire. Neither fire was the type of cozy campfire a cowboy might sit beside.

He grasped the paperback. So far, he hadn't made it past the copyright page. He fluffed his pillows, leaned back, and began reading in chapter one.

He was on L'Amour's trail to peach meadow, lost in the melting frost at the base of the red-orange Vermilion Cliffs with deer feeding in the forest glades, when a knock came to his door.

"Come in."

Jane. Alarm on her face.

"The missing rhinestone. Martin … Amy. If Cecelia gets to him ... I don't know what to do. Disaster's about to strike."

Her words all ran together. So much for finding out the fate of the five-pronged buck spotted by L'Amour's protagonist. Robert set *The Trail to Peach Meadow* back on the nightstand with one hand and held up the palm of his other hand.

"Slow down. Take a deep breath. I'm not following."

"Martin sent Amy a text to meet him in twenty minutes behind the greenhouse. Cecelia saw the message before Amy, took the phone, and left. She's ready to hurt somebody, namely Martin. And if Arnold or Rhoda finds out … I can think of all kinds of ways this could go down and none of them are good."

"Maybe she's gone to get Arnold," Robert said.

"I looked in the main hall. Arnold is engrossed in the movie with Phillip, Evan, and Darin. Martin is gone, and Cecelia is not in her room. As angry as she looked … we need to keep her from doing something crazy."

"It's possible she'll confront him, and he'll see the error of his ways without disturbing everyone else. The greenhouse is off the main path. When I was gathering wood, I discovered another way to approach the back of the greenhouse without being noticed."

Robert stepped back into his shoes and shoved his pistol in the waistband behind his back.

"Do you have to bring a gun?"

"I'd rather have it and not need it than need it and not have it."

CHAPTER FIFTEEN

Jane followed Robert on the path behind the woodshed where they could approach the greenhouse from the opposite side of the main trail. Moonlight reflected from the dark panes of the glass structure. At the sound of voices, Robert pressed his fingers to his lips and tugged Jane into the dark shadows of the trees.

"...behind the greenhouse. Is that your equivalent to meet me in the prop room where we can work on our performance without being interrupted?" Cecelia's voice.

Martin answered. "Ease up now. You don't have to hold a gun on me to make your point. You know I'm attracted to notable talent."

In the moonlight, Jane made out Cecelia's profile holding a gun on Martin, who stood about six feet away from her.

"Attracted? Is that what you call seducing young, impressionable girls?"

"No. No. Amy and I … we're just acting. Performing. You know how it goes."

"Oh, I know all right. I was a fool. A young fool. And you were a scumbag who took advantage. I'll not have you use Amy. I ought to have you arrested."

"Arrested? You forget I covered for you and staged the burglary when you killed Veronica."

Jane gasped, and Robert jammed his hand over her mouth.

"She held a gun on me." Cecelia's voice was shaky.

"You shot her and left her to die," Martin said.

"I didn't shoot. She did. The bullet hit the table."

"And now you're holding a gun on me."

"We struggled. The gun fired. She fell and bumped her head. It was an accident."

"If you shoot me, it will appear you shot again in the heat of the moment," Martin said.

"Again? I ...what are you talking about? You're confusing me."

"Authorities will believe you've blocked what happened from your mind."

"Veronica was shot? No way. She grabbed me; the gun fired but didn't hit her. She fell. You saw her." Cecelia whined. "It was an accident."

"And I covered for you and staged the burglary."

"I'm sick of the cover-up. I'd rather tell all to keep you away from Amy."

"She's above the age of consent. I'm breaking no law."

"Oh, but you are. You are Amy's father." Cecelia hissed the words.

"What?" The word came out of Martin's mouth like a gunshot. "But … the money. The abortion."

"I threw the money away. You're the father only by virtue of biology. Arnold is her father in every sense of the word that matters."

"Does Arnold know?"

"If he does, he's never let on or let it stand in the way of loving her. He's the best thing that happened to me and I can't have you carry this any further with Amy." She waved the gun at Martin.

He held up his hands and took a step toward Cecelia.

"More killing won't help."

Cecelia let the gun drop down to her side and began to sob.

"Lay down the gun and let's figure this out."

Suddenly Rhoda stepped out of the shadows, grabbed the gun and smacked Martin on the side of his head. He crumpled to the ground.

Jane was a spectator in a crime movie. She grabbed Robert's arm. He held up his hand to remain quiet.

"He wants to figure things out," Rhoda said. "That's a joke. There's nothing to figure out. He's a philandering fool. And you, Cecelia, have finally given me my way out."

"Wha … what are you talking about?"

"He had you convinced you were responsible for Veronica's death when she fell. You weren't responsible. He shot her." Rhoda kicked at Martin's still form.

Robert whispered to Jane. "Stay here and pray. I'm going to circle behind Rhoda."

Rhoda gestured with the gun as she talked. "He enlisted me to help make the scene look like another burglary, because the two of us were perfecting break-ins. You see, I was pregnant. And we had a plan. Stage neighborhood burglaries. Give Veronica a gun. Since she is freaked out, she ends up shot by her own gun in a tragic turn of events. Your scuffle with Veronica played out perfectly for us."

"We thought we were free." Rhoda let out a strange, garbled sound. "What a laugh. We were imprisoned. Holding each other hostage with our secret. Now, I discover another joke on me." Rhoda pointed at Martin lying on the ground with the gun. "Know what he told me?"

Cecelia shook her head slowly.

"You begged Martin to loan you the money for an abortion because you were pregnant with Arnold's baby." She put the tip of her shoe under Martin's cheek, lifting his head, then let it drop.

Jane strained to keep Rhoda in view.

"Lies all lies and here's another. The enraged mother of Amy shoots Martin and then herself. The classic murder suicide and I play the grieving betrayed wife."

Snap

A fallen tree branch beneath Jane's foot gave way. She fell to her knees. When she looked up, Rhoda had the gun trained on her. Fear masked any pain from the rough tree bark biting into her legs. Martin remained still. Rhoda motioned Jane to stand beside Cecelia.

"You classmates don't quit, do you?" Moonlight glinted in Rhoda's crazed eyes.

Jane's pulse pounded. Where was Robert?

"Now I have more to explain," Rhoda said.

"Rhoda," Jane said, "we're on the same side, don't you see? If Martin shot Veronica. He needs to take the blame."

"No, it's you who doesn't see. I was an accessory. I've waited eighteen years."

Sweat trickled down Jane's forehead, burning her eyes. She didn't dare move to wipe it away. Rhoda's index finger loosened on the trigger when she talked and tightened when she went silent. Jane had to keep her talking.

"How will you explain away three deaths?"

"Explanations are no problem—I can come up with something. You got in the way, trying to stop poor Cecelia from shooting Martin."

Rhoda rocked back on her heels.

Robert must be having trouble making his way through the woods and underbrush. *Stall.*

"Rhoda, Martin should take the blame. You've paid the price of staying with him for eighteen years. Don't let all the waiting be for nothing."

"It won't be." A barely perceptible moan came from Martin. "You first, dear." She lowered the gun, pointing it at his temple. "Time to face the music." A sadistic laugh bubbled in her throat. "Get it, face the music?"

"I get it." Robert leaped at her from behind. The gun fired into the dirt as he wrestled her to the ground and pinned her arms beneath her. "Jane, call 911. One murder is enough."

~

Jane, her muscles spent, sat next to Robert at the dining table as everyone tried to process what had happened.

Deputies from the local sheriff's office had taken Martin and Rhoda into custody. Robert, Jane, and Cecelia had given statements, using an unoccupied room in the lodge for questioning. Robert, working with the detective, also took Cecelia's statement regarding the cold case and was able to tie the clues from the 2002 investigations together.

Rosemary grasped the coffee mug sitting in front of her, "I'm having a hard time accepting Mr. Sing murdered his wife."

"Murders are often committed by those who are thought to be incapable." Robert said.

"What gets me is Rhoda was in on the killing of Veronica and had been in on the neighborhood burglaries," Arnold said.

"Staging break-ins was their answer to getting

Veronica out of the way because Rhoda was pregnant," Robert said.

"Cecelia, you went to the Singletary house because Martin was to give you money?" Evan asked.

Cecelia bit at her lip and looked at Arnold. Arnold had nothing but compassion in his eyes. Amy sat next to him with her head down. Cecelia glanced at Jane, her eyes a plea to not broadcast the whole truth of why Martin gave her the four- hundred dollars.

Jane interceded. "Mr. Singletary heard you had some extra expenses and—"

"I remember," Rosemary said. "Your car broke down and we were all upset having to buy white dresses that would be covered by the graduation gown."

"Yes. Mr. Singletary offered me a loan. He gave me a key. I was to meet him at his house and wait in the kitchen."

"I get the picture," Darin said. "With all the break-ins in the neighborhood, Veronica must have freaked out and thought you were a burglar."

Cecelia twisted her hands together. "We struggled. The gun went off and hit the table leg and she bumped her head."

More pieces of the puzzle came together as Cecelia talked. The struggle she described would account for the chipped fingernail, and rhinestone from her pin mixed in the peaches at the murder scene.

"She lay there on the floor with a cut on her head." Cecelia said. "I couldn't tell how badly she was hurt.

Martin insisted I keep quiet, and he'd make it appear Veronica had walked in on a burglary. I didn't know what I was doing. I took the money and ran. When I got to the bridge at the river, the gravity of the situation hit me. I didn't want the money. I threw it over the bridge."

"Four one-hundred-dollar bills?" Evan asked.

Cecelia nodded and blew her nose. Evan looked at Phillip. "That explains the money we found. And certain people," he looked at Robert, "thought it was suspicious."

Robert winced and nodded.

"The suspicion led Principal Jones to advise me to join the military," Phillip said. "I'd done nothing wrong when I found the hundred-dollar bill, but I'd built a reputation of doing things that were wrong. I'm a better man for going into the military."

"I'll say." Rosemary reached up and kissed his cheek.

"Mr. Singletary was mean to let you think you were at fault all these years." Caroline's remark elicited a sob out of Amy, whose long hair partially obscured her face. Caroline patted her hand. "It must be hard to take all this in, with him teaching you to sing and all."

Arnold handed Cecelia his handkerchief and she blew her nose. "I thought she died from hitting her head on the table, not a gunshot."

"Normal police procedure. The details of the death were not given out," Robert said. "I'll tell you what I'm at liberty to share."

Thankfully, Robert took over. Jane's friends were naturally inquisitive, but their questions were making Cecelia uneasy. She would not want anyone to know Amy was Martin's child or that she had accepted money to have her baby aborted.

"Rhoda was pregnant with Martin's baby. Their original plan was to stage burglaries in the neighborhood to make Veronica nervous, give her a gun, and then use it against her later. With Veronica gone, they could marry and give their baby a name."

"When Cecelia and Veronica's struggle left Veronica unconscious, Rhoda and Martin entered into a sinister pact. Martin shot and killed his wife and Rhoda helped stage the burglary. Rid of Veronica, they were free to marry but imprisoned by each other's complicity."

"Tonight, after Martin's musical presentation …" Robert hesitated and glanced toward Amy, "… Cecelia went to speak to Martin. Jane was worried. We followed and overheard Martin telling Cecelia the truth about what happened to Veronica. Rhoda, who had apparently reached the end of her patience with their pact, appeared and picked up Cecelia's gun. She was willing to risk killing Cecelia and Martin and make it appear as a homicide-suicide."

"She didn't figure on Robert hearing everything and taking the gun from her," Jane said.

"What happens to them now?" Amy's voice cracked.

"From their confessions, there is enough to charge

them with murder. They will be held for extradition to Valley County Sheriff's Office where they will await trial."

Amy buried her face in her hands.

Jane swallowed her discomfort and hoped Amy would never know her father was Martin Singletary.

Arnold hugged his daughter. "All of us make mistakes; what's important is to learn from them and move on." He slid his chair back, the legs rubbing against the wood floor. He stood behind Amy and gently patted her shoulders and nodded to Cecelia. "Let's go for a walk." The three left arm in arm.

Letting Cecelia believe she was responsible for Veronica's death was a terrible burden Martin placed on her. He allowed her to think he had sacrificed and covered for her.

And what about Arnold? Did he know Amy was not his? Jane's assumption had always been that their quick marriage was due to pregnancy, and Arnold was the father. If he suspected otherwise, he never let it show. He had always adored Cecelia and seemed to adore Amy as well.

Jane watched as they departed. Walking through the great room, a halo of light cast by the wagon wheel chandelier covered Arnold with his arms wrapped around his girls. Whether Arnold suspected Martin was Amy's father or not didn't matter. He was her father in every other sense of the word.

"Arnold is right," Phillip said. "We do need to move

on."

"I'll drink to that, sweet pea, if I had something to drink." Rosemary turned over her coffee cup and let the drips fall into her other hand.

"We better lay off the coffee. It's nearly midnight and we still have a sunrise wedding." Jane used her cheery voice. "Sit tight and I'll bring water."

"What I want to know ..." Evan started posing another question to Robert.

"I'll help with the water." Darin stood and followed Jane.

Jane opened the refrigerator and pulled out bottled water.

"So Jane, what do say about applying for the archive job in Montgomery?" Darin asked.

The cool temperature from the refrigerator was not nearly as cold as the way Darin's question struck Jane. "I'd say we just experienced a monumental trauma finding out our teacher and his current wife conspired to murder his former wife. Then covered it up while letting one of our best friends suffer for eighteen years, thinking she was responsible. *And* I can't believe you'd bring up making application for a job right now."

"Well … sure. But like you say, that was eighteen years ago—ancient history. This opening closes in three days. We've got to be realists."

"Yes, we do. And let me tell you what I am a realist about at the moment. I am put off by your wanting to make amends and pretending to think of me and my interests. When you encouraged me to apply for the historian job, you left something out. If I took the job and we reattached, you would once again be a member of the Heart of Montgomery club—the membership you lost when Cynthia divorced you."

"The divorce was mutual."

"Whatever. The divorce still ended your membership unless you came up with twelve grand."

"Hold up. Who told you that?"

"A lady named Rhoda, who is not only familiar with the inner workings of the club but with manipulation and betrayal."

"Well, she doesn't know how I feel about you."

"Darin, I need to know, not Rhoda. We are meant to be friends, not lovers. I agree with Arnold too. We both need to move on. No more talk about the Montgomery job because we have more important jobs—you as best man and me as maid of honor."

CHAPTER SIXTEEN

At 4:15, the alarm sounded. After restless dozing, Jane sprung out of bed, showered, and slipped into the simple, red sundress she'd chosen for the wedding and hurried down the hall to check on Rosemary.

Rosemary opened the door to her knock. "I was going to ask if you needed any help, but I see you're dressed already."

Rosemary wore a white street length dress with a sweetheart neckline. "You know me. Miss Independent."

"Soon to be Mrs."

"Yup. How do you like my shoes?"

Rosemary planted the toe of her right foot next to the left to show them off. Her antics made Jane laugh and were the best medicine for the tensions settled into her neck and shoulders after last night's ordeal. "Only you could accessorize your wedding dress with white polka-dotted red pumps and look perfect."

"I thought they would look good with my glasses."

"The bride is supposed to be the show."

Rosemary fluffed one side of her thick red-hair, glamour girl style. "Doing my part as a Shooting Star for a wedding that shines. But there is one thing you can do for me."

"Name it."

Rosemary grabbed both of Jane's hands. "Pray for me and Phil."

"I'd be honored." She and Rosemary bowed. "Lord, we join hands in agreement, asking for your blessing over the long-awaited marriage of Rosemary and Phillip. Take them into your hands and let joy, peace, and contentment dwell within them. As they become a family, may they each bring their best self to the other with commitment and faith. Amen."

"Amen, sister. Thank you."

Jane gave her a hug. "You've got this. I'm going to check on everyone else. Stay put until you get your cue."

Downstairs, Cecelia and Amy were setting up the wedding breakfast buffet.

"Did you see the plastic toasting cups in the kitchen?" Jane asked.

"Got them right here." Amy held up the package.

Jane was thankful to see smiles on both of their faces. The smell of yeasty bread and cinnamon woke up her taste buds. "Something smells delicious."

"Your delivery order came right on time."

In the kitchen, Evan and Caroline were slicing the sweet-smelling brioche. "Looks like you two have everything under control."

"Do you want the cut fruit on platters or in individual cups?" Caroline asked.

"Platters will be fine." Jane was pleased all was going smoothly but felt useless.

Outside, Arnold had his tablet strategically placed, ready to open the zoom link for virtual wedding guests.

Robert, looking sharp in a blue sport coat and slacks, stood beside the CD player.

Jane joined him. "I see you're ready to punch the play button for the opening and closing music.

"Yes, ma'am."

They stood silent for a moment, admiring the gray, hazy hint of daybreak. A bird tweeted as the sky lightened and began taking on the orange and pink tinges of dawn.

"God's painting," Robert said.

"New every morning."

"Um … looks like Rosemary and Phil will be blessed with a beautiful sunrise."

The brush of Robert's shoulder sent an unexpected thrill to her heart.

At exactly 5:15, Darin and Phillip took their places beside Arnold at the edge of the terrace.

Cecelia signaled that Rosemary was in place.

Robert pressed the CD player button, giving life to

The Beatles singing "Here Comes the Sun." He lifted his brows and wiggled his index finger as if seeking affirmation. Jane held her bouquet and gave him a nod of approval as she stepped forward and took her place on the other side of Arnold.

Cecelia opened the terrace door, and Rosemary stepped out. The bride radiated joy. Jane could almost discern rays like sunshine streaming from her.

After the traditional words of the wedding ceremony, Arnold gave Phillip and Rosemary the opportunity to make their own special vows to one another.

Phillip spoke first. "Like Ike in the *Runaway Bride* movie, I believe you want a guy who will wake you up at dawn. A guy who is bursting to talk to you. A guy who can't wait another minute to find out what you'll say. Rosemary, I will be that guy for you."

Rosemary pushed her red framed glasses on top of her head and said, "Somebody hand me a tissue."

Cecelia passed a tissue to Jane, who passed it to Rosemary whose tears trailed her cheeks.

Wiping away the tears, Rosemary said, "Sweet pea, I look forward to you waking me up to hear what I have to say, but it can be a little later than dawn." She repositioned her glasses and grabbed both of Phillip's hands. "Phillip Lance Randolph, as a member of the Shooting Stars we established a wish. Like a star that gives a brief look as it streaks across the sky, we wished to have a sneak peek at the one we would marry. I caught a glimpse of you in the high school parking lot and like a brand on a cow's hindquarters, you seared my heart for keeps. I love you for all you have been, for all you are, and for all you are yet to be."

The sun popped above the mountain ridge turning the rosy dawn to a golden yellow and highlighted the newlyweds' kiss.

On cue, Robert played Sonny & Cher's "I Got You Babe". Rosemary twirled around, the skirt of her dress flaring, and she clicked the heels of her red polka-dotted shoes like Dorothy in the *Wizard of Oz*. Phillip gave her an adoring grin.

Jane followed behind them, escorted by Darin. "Do you think you've caught a glimpse of your one and only?" he asked her.

"The jury is still out."

~

The group gathered in the great room for the breakfast buffet. Amy, exhibiting the resiliency afforded youth, busied herself texting. Robert engaged with Phillip in conversation. Jane went to the buffet table and sipped some champagne, letting the bubbles tickle her throat.

Darin, who chatted with Caroline, motioned to Jane to join them. "Listen to what Caroline has been telling me. Did you know she was a Capstone Woman at 'Bama?"

"I did."

Caroline's eyes twinkled. "I heard Darin was disappointed about losing membership in that

Montgomery club and was telling him he should check out the Crimson Tide Foundation."

Darin blurted. "They are looking for a senior level financial planner. The job includes membership in the exclusive Champions Club."

"I still have connections," Caroline said, "I could put in a good word for you. It is a great place to network with loyal alumni, fans and friends who give gobs of financial support to the Athletics Department."

Jane cast Darin a smile. "Sounds promising. Is gobs a measurable financial term?"

"No, but the visual works for me." He turned back to Caroline. "I'll take your good word on my behalf."

The weight of hurt and regret Jane had felt over the years by getting dropped by Darin lifted. She could see and accept him as a guy who looked to societal acceptance to feel secure and grounded. And Caroline? Maybe Evan had made a good choice for the kindergarten.

"Hey." Rosemary grabbed Jane's elbow. "I need to talk to you." She steered Jane to a quiet spot beside the fireplace.

"I'm breaking tradition."

"You say that as if it's something new."

Rosemary's laughter spilled over. "My Shooting Star friend, from our *90210* heartthrob picks in our favorite TV show, I got my Dylan. Cecelia has her David. I'm bucking tradition and not taking a chance on tossing this bouquet." She pressed the bridal bouquet into

Jane's hands. "It's yours. You are next in line to get your Brandon." Rosemary wiggled her brows above her red glasses and nodded in Robert's direction.

CHAPTER SEVENTEEN

Jane stared at the calendar on the wall in the investigations office. The days in July were running out. Fourth of July—the normal time to break out the charcoal grills, participate in parades, and close the day, with oohs and aahs over brilliant, crackling fireworks—had been a bust.

The coronavirus beat down this year's carnival spirit. Grocers still had red, white, and blue displays for chips and hot dogs, but Mobile canceled their annual Fourth of July events.

The dampened holiday cheer matched Jane's disheartened mood. Her morning devotion had proclaimed from Proverbs. "*A cheerful heart is good medicine, but a crushed spirit dries up the bones*." That was her problem. She felt crushed like a rock under a sledgehammer, or a flower, raising its head to the sun, only to be smashed by an avalanche.

Not only the pandemic had put a damper on life, but Rosemary's call added to Jane's doldrums. "Hate to be the conveyor of bad news, but the place you put a deposit on in Valleytown fell through. My realtor friend said the current renters, who had first right of refusal, signed a lease to stay another year."

"All my other options have dried up and now my dream cottage choice has been erased."

"The bright side is, you'll get back the two-hundred-dollar deposit you put down. I'd invite you to live with Phil and me, except we're in a one-bedroom apartment until we are able to build. We could always fix up the storage space over the café for you."

"You are sweet to offer. But with the start of school only weeks away, I'll rent an efficiency at the 'Bama Motor Inn on the highway."

"It's all about open-and-closed doors. A place like the lake cottage you found outside town is for you. I can feel it in my bones. But it's just not for you right now. There will be a better time. You're wondering which way to turn. But if you seek God for direction, he'll show you the way. You prayed for me, my friend, now I'm praying for you."

"Dear Lord, help my friend, Jane. She doesn't know what to do or where to turn, but you do. And I'm requesting a rush order, 'cause she needs you to point her to the right course ASAP. Amen and thank you Jesus."

Rosemary's prayer was good medicine and cheered Jane's heart. She should look for God's direction and do her part and face facts.

Her world, here in Mobile, was coming to a close. No more group therapy, no more PI work with Robert. She shoved the file drawer closed with a bang. Once the calendar page flipped, she'd be staring at the date she would become officially homeless.

The two desks, shelves, coffee table, and file cabinets that comprised Robert's office were the only home she had now. Here she had a place to unwind and be herself, to laugh at the craziness of life, admit she was not perfect, and recognize no one else was either.

The office was where she made memories shared with Robert during the cases they'd worked. But now it seemed Robert was interested in the cold case job, and it was time for her to take her next steps.

She had to return to Valleytown. Her idea of a valley had once been a green pasture beside a brook with water trickling over the stones. The setting was a restful and restorative place where God's care was evident.

But valleys could also be inhospitable locations with deep shadows and restricted views of what lies ahead.

Green pastures and dark valleys, she had seen both. Her year with the agency began with insecurities, but Robert—the man who saved her from drug traffickers, shielded her in a burning building, rescued her from a crazed woman with a .38, and scaled a wall for her—had stuck with her. Something no man in her life had ever done.

Now Jane faced unknown territory. There would be no more frightened kindergarteners and parents needing her coaxing and calming skills. An unfamiliar classroom and unprepared lessons lay obscured in the shadows of her path to the future.

What she could see clearly was the stack of papers in the *To be Filed* section of her current desk organizer. On her way to sort the pile, the office phone rang.

"Hi Jane." Vance Freed's cheery voice came on the line. "Congratulations are in order."

"Why?"

"For solving the murder case."

"Robert is due those congratulations."

"Not according to him, but the big deal is those responsible are in custody. I think the husband is banking on spousal testimonial privilege."

Still confounded over the arrests of Martin and Rhoda, Jane did agree that justice must be served. "Will spousal privilege work? They weren't married at the time of the murder."

"Good question. The lawyers and courts will have to hash out the answer. Is Robert around?"

"He drove to Montgomery for a meeting pertaining to the case. He'll probably call you or stop by."

"I'd like to see him, but I'm working a case in Crenshaw County. I figured the department head would want to talk to him. Robert is making a name for himself."

"I'm glad." A pang of guilt hit, thinking of how she'd accused him of using her friends to restore his law enforcement reputation. "He deserves the recognition."

"You should take a bow, too. Have you set up an interview yet?"

"Me? What interview?"

"For the curator job."

Was he talking about the job Darin had mentioned? "I'm not following you."

"Maybe with all the excitement of the arrests, Robert failed to mention it. The archives department head likes your credentials and wants you to fill out an application so an interview can be arranged."

"Vance, I have no clue what you are talking about."

"The Curator of Education job at the museum in Montgomery. Robert asked me to check into it for you."

"When did he do that?"

"The day he picked up the cold case file. Say ... I thought you knew. I may be spoiling a surprise."

Robert had been checking into a job for her? He should have talked to her first. "It is a surprise."

"The museum is pretty nice and with your education experience and all ..."

Vance's voice became background noise. Robert recommended her for a job and didn't tell her? He knew she was supposed to return to her teaching job. He also was aware of her love for history and research. Was he looking for something else for her to do in case she didn't return to teaching? Was it a given she would not stay on with him at the agency? Did he want her to leave?

"... gotta go. Have him call me when he gets in."

"Sure. I will."

She hung up the phone and slumped into her desk chair. Crushed again. Robert took it on himself to look into a job for her and didn't tell her. What was it with her and the men in her life? They all disappointed her. Her dad and brother had left her behind. Evan and Darin wanted her around for what she could offer them. And now Robert worked behind her back on a job in case she backed out of teaching. Not a bad idea. Then he could hire someone with law enforcement experience. But he should have talked to her first.

She opened the drawer to her desk and pulled out the badge encased in the leather waist clip holder. She'd thought the PI shield with her name meant she was proving capable, but maybe not.

Her prayer had been for God to make clear the direction she should take. Was this news something God was trying to show her? If so, why did it feel like she was being shown the door?

She returned the badge to the drawer.

The office door opened, and Robert came in all smiles. "I see you're tackling the piled-up paperwork."

"One thing I'm good for."

"There's lots more than one."

"Like a museum job?"

His brows shot up. Caught, but he recovered with a knowing smile. "Ah. Vance must have spilled the beans before I could tell you. I'm aware you fully intend to go back to the elementary school, and I may have been presumptuous, but I asked Vance to check into the job. You were interested enough to run off the job description and the requirements seem to suit you."

She crossed her arms. "Not because you wanted to make certain I had another job in case I waffled on going back to the classroom?"

"What? Why would I do that?"

"Because I'm tough to work with. Think about it. You're constantly having to rescue me from tight spots. And I seem to recall, before our last case, being classified as unceremonious, ungovernable, and underfoot."

"Your words, not mine. Are you finished?"

"Sort of."

~

Robert tossed the folder holding the job offer to work with the cold case unit on his desk. Jane understanding his motives was more important right now. He walked to her desk, sat on the corner, and then leveled his eyes on her. "I thought I taught you to never jump to conclusions. To me your 'uns' are unfathomable, unequaled and unforgettable. I looked into the curator job because I want you to do what you are meant to do."

She pressed her lips together and looked down.

"You are meant to explore, research, and delve into detail. But more than anything, I'd like for you to stay with me at the agency."

Her eyes shot up to meet his. "You would?"

"Of course." He slid from the desk and paced. There was so much he wanted to share, and walking might help the words to come. "Working here, you have added the exceptional ingredient of attention to detail. You held the key to solving the Singletary murder when you spotted the missing rhinestone and tied it to the crime scene evidence. But I can't offer the compensation you deserve. I don't want to hold you back."

He turned to face her. "Asking Vance to find out more about the status of the museum job had been a whim, but Evan changing you to fifth grade could indicate it's time to look at a job change. Maybe our mountaintop experience had less to do with a wedding and more to do with making us take stock in our next steps."

"Maybe." Jane wrinkled her forehead. "I still need to apologize for accusing you of wanting to recover your cop image no matter who it hurt."

"Apologize for the truth? No. I can't deny the idea of solving the murder and boosting my image in law enforcement circles hadn't crossed my mind."

"Nevertheless, according to Vance, your name is receiving acclaim by solving the cold case."

"If my good name is restored, I owe it to you."

"Me?" Jane flicked a dismissive hand wave. "How?"

"Taking a stand for me when others mistrusted me. Giving back is now my turn. Look at this." Robert pulled a paper from his pocket. "I spoke to an administrative assistant in the Department of Archives and History who gave me more information on the proposed curator position. The job is to collaboratively plan and implement programming for school age audiences, includes retirement and health benefits, and best of all because of the pandemic you can work from your home office."

She looked at the paper, but her face didn't light up as he had hoped.

"Sounds wonderful. But ... I don't have a home."

"Don't you have a deposit on a place?"

"I did. A cute cottage on a lake, but Rosemary just called. The people currently renting renewed their lease."

"I'm sorry." He refolded and poked the information sheet back in his pocket. "I thought this might be the ideal solution for you to have your dream job and leave Evan with finding another teacher for fifth grade."

"I admit this job is tempting, but I received my welcome back to school letter. The first day for teachers is in a week, August seventeenth. I'll rent a by-the-week efficiency until I find something else."

"A motel room?" He shook his head and sunk into his desk chair. Her need was twofold. Finding a place to live and a job with benefits.

He opened the folder he'd received that morning with the proposal to join the cold case unit. Return to law enforcement. Wasn't that the desire of his heart? Apparently not, or he would have jumped at the opportunity. He told the department head he'd give it serious thought. And he would.

But his thinking was clouded with the harsh reality of the date fast approaching for Jane to report to school—August 17. Time was running out and there was no stopping it … or was there?

CHAPTER EIGHTEEN

Robert opened the passenger door of his truck.

Jane scooted in, curiosity bugging her. “No hints on where we’re going?”

“Nope.”

“At least tell me if I’m dressed appropriately for the occasion.”

“Jeans and a top are fine. We’ll be out pretty late, but I have an extra jacket if needed.”

Jane frowned. “Why all the mystery?”

“Detectives and mystery go together.”

“Hmm. So do pork and beans but they don’t keep it a secret.”

Robert grinned, cranked his truck, and backed out of the drive at her mother’s house. “I see the realtor still has the sign up in the yard.”

“Hanging the sold banner on the sign gives them

bragging rights, I suppose." The sign was also a constant reminder that in a matter of days the new owners would move in, and she would be living out of a suitcase.

Jane opened Robert's glove box and rummaged through it. Nothing but napkins, ketchup packets and the truck handbook.

"What are you looking for?"

"A clue to where we're going. Detectives and clues also go together."

"You'll see. Relax and enjoy the ride." Robert tilted his head, looking way too satisfied with himself. "The Jane I know will figure it out soon enough."

"The Jane I know needs a hint."

"Just keep your eyes open."

"It's dark out."

"It's supposed to be. That's your first clue."

"Supposed to be … a moonlight boat ride?"

"Sounds lovely, but no."

"Another hint."

"You are one."

"A girl?"

"Yes, and there are two more."

"Two more girls? We're going to see two girls?"

"No. Two of your girlfriends have this in common."

"You're talking about Rosemary and Cecelia? Are we going to Valleytown?"

"Look around you."

They passed a road sign. State Road 59. Wrong way

to Valleytown. "This is the road we used to take to Pine Bluff. Are we going to your hometown?"

"Good detective work. I said you'd figure it out."

"By the time we arrive, it will be close to ten o'clock. Pine Bluff has a nightlife?"

"After we arrive, it will."

"Mr. Grey. You've captured my interest."

Leaving Mobile and Robert had brought her spirits to a low, but his quirky grin gave her a boost of good cheer.

Jane settled into the soft leather seat and breathed in the citrus fragrance of Robert's after shave. She would relax and savor being near this man who had taken her under wing and had planned some kind of surprise for her. They'd traveled this road many times, working on their first big murder case.

She looked out the window and viewed the trees appearing as dark velvet, snuggling around them away from city streetlights. She and Robert had experienced a lot working together. She was going to miss their deliberations over what to include and how to word reports, his dry humor, late night chats, trying to keep each other awake during a surveillance, his rules, dancing in a palace, how he made her feel when they brushed shoulders … and his kiss.

"You're deep in thought." He glanced at her as the headlights from an oncoming car lit the smile that shone in his eyes. She smiled back, and he returned his focus to the road. He understood her and didn't press.

They were comfortable in each other's presence. Non-silent silence? Rosemary's words. Look for the one who understands you. Don't settle.

When they reached Pine Bluff, Jane straightened in her seat. Stores were closed and all was quiet. No surprise. The only illumination was streetlights and the ground lights shining on the silver-domed courthouse.

"Now what?"

"Now we press on to our destination." Robert took the county road leading away from town toward Summerfield Road. They passed the wayside park, once a crime scene, the bio-energy corporation where arrests were made and kept going.

"Are we going to your Uncle Jim's?"

His headlights lit up the mailbox with the Grey family name attached. "Yes, we are," he said, turning into the drive. "I spoke to Uncle Jim last night, and he's with their motorhome club circled up in the Black Hills. I told him I'd check on the place."

Jane took in the old familiar scenery. An exterior light partially lit the farmhouse, nesting in the shadows of an old oak tree. Behind the house stood a hay barn. Jane could detect the outline of a tractor inside. The moon reflected on the small lake. The guest cottage where Jane had stayed while they worked to clear the local sheriff charged with murder was barely visible.

She'd spent some pleasant mornings on the front porch reading her Bible and watching the rising sun burn away the mist hugging the water. "It's beautiful out here away from the city lights, with the wide-open sky."

"That's the whole idea."

"Idea? I'm still in the dark."

"Stargazing." He cut his eyes to her. "Miss Shooting Star, how does a nighttime picnic watching the August Perseids meteor shower sound?"

She blinked, and a shaft of delight ran through her. "Fantastic."

He turned on his full out grin, which she'd learned meant he was up to something.

"I pulled a Jane and researched the proper procedure. We can use the barn to block the moonlight in order to see the stars better. Come on. Help me get the blanket and basket out of the back."

"I can't believe you planned all this."

"You aren't the only one who can organize and carry out a plan, though I dare say your menu might have been better. Peanut butter and jelly sandwiches with sliced apples and bottled water is our evening fare."

"Sounds perfect to me."

Jane stared after him as he spread the blanket, and a pang of regret touched her heart. In a few days, she would be leaving this man who had become such a part of her life. Like Robert angling a way to block out the moon, she'd managed to block out the fact. But the truth was the moon was still out there beyond the barn, and she was still scheduled to leave for Valleytown. Would they even see each other again? They'd made no plans.

"Are you just going to stand there? Set the basket down."

She needed to block the sad thoughts, or she'd spoil the evening.

They sat down and munched on their supper. The nutty flavor from the sandwich and the crisp tang of the apples pulled up memories long forgotten of a backyard camp out under the stars with Cecelia and Rosemary. Gazing at the sky, she asked, "Tell me what you learned in your research."

"The Perseids are prolific meteor showers which appear to come from inside the constellation Perseus. The meteor shower peaks on warm August nights and is active from mid- July to late August. To see them, you must find a dark open sky, spread out a blanket and watch patiently. Hence I chose here."

He lifted the water bottle to his mouth, then stopped and pointed with the neck of the bottle. "Look."

A glittering celestial spray streaked over the night sky. "Incredible. A cool summer night is an amazing way to close out a hot summer day."

Robert stretched out on his back and clasped his hands beneath his head. "The shooting star showers come in spurts with a lull in between, so you are supposed to settle in and watch the show."

"Shooting stars remind me of God scrutinizing our comings and goings from above."

"God's omniscient eyesight," Robert said. "At the

lodge, I looked into the piercing eye of an eagle statue. Eagles have more keen eyesight than humans. Think of how much more God sees and understands the best direction for us."

"I've been praying he'd clue me in on what to do next." Jane nodded toward the little cottage beside the lake that shimmered like a sheet of polished black granite. "Returning here is like coming home. At least what I imagine it might feel like if I had such a thing as a family homestead. The house I had hoped to rent in Valleytown reminded me of this place, so the disappointment doubled when the deal fell through."

"Jane." Robert turned to face her. "I checked with my uncle, and he said you can stay here."

"That's sweet, but this must be three hours from Valleytown."

"Two hours if you take I-65. You could stay in the motel during the week and come here on weekends. If teaching fifth grade is what you really want to do, at least you'd have a home base."

Jane stared at the cottage with the lake. Was staying here possible? "The job you checked on for me. Would it matter how far away my home office was? I mean … do you think I'd have a chance to get the job?"

"The department head told Vance he wanted you to apply, and the assistant I talked to said you'd be a good match with your classroom experience." His words came in an excited rush. "Programs they want developed include virtual tours, distance learning, and a traveling unit to take exhibits to schools. Where you live and your hours can be flexible. And you can stargaze every night. Think about it."

"I will." Jane leaned back on her elbows mesmerized by the streaks of light darting through the clear black sky. Suddenly, a larger glowing meteor appeared.

"There's a fireball." Robert rolled to his side, facing her and a fireball of heat raced over Jane at his nearness. "Reminds me of Rosemary and your friends at the lodge. Though things were intense at times, I almost envied the benefits of camaraderie you must have shared singing together in high school."

"Our group, admittedly an odd mix, was like a family. A family I made after my parents divorced."

"When you said you had no home. I thought of Pine Bluff and my privilege of having roots here. This has been Grey farmland for three generations. Uncle Jim wants me to take over the land, so it remains in the family."

Jane sat up, hugging her knees close. Surveying their surroundings, she breathed in the night air. "What did you tell him?"

"I'd think about it. And … well, I not only wanted you to see the shooting stars tonight but to …" His voice cracked. He cleared his throat and sat up. "I made a mistake hiring you."

Jane's stomach lurched.

"I have avoided commitments and attachments because loss is painful. But when I met you, something nudged me to hire you. I messed up, because now I face the pain of losing you at the end of the summer."

"But that's been the plan all along—the job was temporary…"

"Falling in love with you was not included in the plan."

"… and I'd return to … Wait. What?"

Robert stood and looked down at her. "I love you, Jane Carson. I can't deny it. I told myself that I could be content with friendship. But no matter how much I've tried to fight it," he pointed to the sky, "like those crazy stars that fell on Alabama, I've fallen for you."

He seemed exasperated. More flashes streaked the sky in succession. He drew in a breath and let it out before continuing.

"Life is a series of moments; flashes of time and I want to spend my future moments with you. Teach or don't teach, work for the museum or don't work, continue as a PI or quit. I don't care. Whatever, however, wherever, whenever, makes no difference as long as you are with me. My roots can be your roots. I don't know if I measure up to that Brandon heartthrob character of yours or what the Shooting Stars Club members would say about me—"

Jane stood up and pressed her finger to his lips. "The Shooting Stars would say you're talking too much." His sweet breath and sweet words were a whisper away.

When they kissed, the sensation flooded her body, starting with her toes. He lifted her off the ground, and tingles went straight to her head. Then came a new realization. She pushed away. "You're the guy."

He brushed hair away from her face and gave her a puzzled look.

"The guy I saw in the principal's office. You went to the office and talked to the secretary during the murder investigation. Dark suit? Blue tie? Badge at your waist?"

Robert nodded.

"Don't you see? It was you. The official Shooting Star wish is that each of us glimpse of our future love." She poked him in the chest. "I saw you. I even wrote about you in my diary. Can you believe it?"

"With you around, I've come to believe many things."

"We have to revise your rule list."

"What? Why?"

"Number four, about resisting the urge to become personally involved."

"The rule applies to potential witnesses."

Robert traced his finger over her brows, nose, cheeks and came to her lips, making her entire body go weak. "We're witnessing shooting stars."

He lifted her chin and pressed his finger to her lips. "Now you're talking too much."

He was right. No talking necessary. Just a prayer of thanks for the peaceful feeling she'd been longing for. She was not doomed to settle. They kissed. A soft, tender kiss.

Drawing into his comforting scent, she snuggled against his chest, rested her head on his shoulder and gazed at the splashes of light dashing across the sky. Jane might not know her exact next steps but with Robert's support and his arms around her, together they would find the best path.

With summer's end, the seasons of Jane's year of excitement and mystery as a PI with Robert had come to a close. The breeze stirred the flowers in the meadow on Uncle Jim's farm. A sense of knowing touched her soul. And as she rose on tiptoes to capture Robert's smile and his lips, the summer blossoms whispered of hope for them to share more seasons to come.

A FREE GIFT FOR YOU

Sign up for Sally Jo's News

And receive a free short story,

The Winter Solstice Bride

A marriage of convenience in 1907 begins the union

of an intriguing founding family in the small Florida coastal town of Hamilton Harbor. The legacy of this couple provides lessons of faith and love for the future in the Hamilton Harbor Legacy Series.

Go to

https://sallyjopitts.com

for your free story.

Did you enjoy the book?

Could you leave an online review? It's the best thing you can do for an author next to purchasing the book! It doesn't have to be long. Giving a rating and writing a simple sentence will do.

Amazon- https://www.amazon.com/author/sallyjopitts

Bookbub- https://www.bookbub.com/profile/sally-jo-pitts?list=author_books

Goodreads- https://www.goodreads.com/author/show/18207570.Sally_Jo_Pitts

Thanks!

Dear Reader,

I hope you enjoyed the fourth book in the Seasons of Mystery series with Private Investigators Robert Grey and Jane Carson. When I first started planning the summer book, I envisioned a high school reunion—either Robert's or Jane's—on a cruise ship. However, the *Winter Deception* storyline pinpointed the year as 2019, which placed *Spring Betrayal* and *Summer Cover-Up* in 2020. So … I had to deal with the global COVID-19 pandemic.

I created an isolated mountain retreat where a small group of high school friends could reunite and quarantine for a wedding. Though Eaglemont is fictitious, the location is set near the Alabama side of Lookout Mountain—the gateway to the Appalachians.

The lodge layout is patterned after Bald Rock Lodge in Cheaha State Park, Alabama. The idea of hand hewn local rocks fitted together on the outside of the building and words of wisdom inscribed in stone around the property was sparked by The Grove Park Inn in Asheville, North Carolina. I tossed in a cold case murder along with romantic conflict and from there the story unfolded.

Solving mysteries in this series has highlighted the

ever-changing seasons. Autumn, winter, spring, and summer each bring a fresh start, flowing one after another into the future.

Just as Robert and Jane seek God's next steps for their future, I pray that you as the reader embrace and find the purpose for the season in which you find yourself.

In my novels, I like to incorporate food in some way. I chose Yummy Bars to include in a scene in *Summer Cover-Up*. The dessert was first introduced to me by one of my friend's mom's when I was in high school. The recipe is at the end of this book.

I love to hear from readers. You can connect with me at www.sallyjopitts.com where I share recipes and more about books I love.

Wishing you blessings,

Sally Jo

The Seasons of Mystery Series

Autumn Vindication (book #1)

Initially working a voter fraud case, Robert and Jane find themselves in the middle of a homicide, and their client is the prime suspect.

Winter Deception (book #2)

Christmas at the historical antebellum plantation could have provided a restful holiday ...
if it weren't for the murder.

Spring Betrayal (book #3)

Grey Investigations must untangle a royal mess before a revolution overtakes a Caribbean monarchy.

Summer Cover-Up (book #4)

A wedding party is quarantined at a mountain lodge—
And one of them may be a cold case killer.

Additional audio links at
https://sallyjopitts.com/mysterybooks

Acknowledgments

Due special thanks are Marcia Lahti, Regina Smeltzer, and Jodi Janz for their in-depth content and grammatical critique of the manuscript.

To readers Tommy Vaughan-Birch and Tammie Shaw, thank you for your encouragement and recommendations.

I am grateful to Cynthia Hickey of Winged Publications, who believed in this project and suggested the name for the Seasons of Mystery series.

Yummy Bars

½ c. butter, melted

1 ½ c. graham cracker crumbs

1 c. semi-sweet chocolate chips

1 1/3 c. shredded coconut

1 can sweetened condensed milk

Grease a 9 X 13 baking pan with cooking spray. Line with parchment paper. In a medium bowl, mix butter and graham cracker crumbs. Press into the prepared baking dish to form a crust. Sprinkle chocolate chips, then coconut over the crust. Pour sweetened condensed milk evenly over coconut. Bake at 350 degrees for 25 minutes. Cool and cut into bars. (May also layer in 1 c. butterscotch chips and 1 c. chopped pecans or walnuts.)

About the Author

Sally Jo Pitts has had a career in private investigations, lie detection, high school guidance counseling and taught in the field of marriage and family living for over twenty years. Now she combines her detective and education experience to bring inspirational fiction to the printed page. She is author of the Hamilton Harbor Legacy romance series and the Seasons of Mystery series. Residing in north Florida with her schnauzer Gibbs, Sally Jo enjoys hot mochas, old movies, and creating stories from scribbled notes that clutter her house. More about the author and things she investigates can be found at www.sallyjopitts.com

A SPECIAL OFFER

Sign up for Forget Me Not Romances newsletter and receive a special gift compiled from Forget Me Not Authors!

Join our FB pages to keep up on our most current news!

Forget Me Not Romances Readers and Authors

Take Me Away Books

Winged Publications

Soaring Beyond

Made in the USA
Columbia, SC
18 May 2025

58093607R00183